JURASSIC WORLD

CHAOS THEORY

Published by Scholastic Australia in 2024.

Scholastic Australia Pty Limited
PO Box 579 Gosford NSW 2250
ABN 11 000 614 577
www.scholastic.com.au

Part of the Scholastic Group
Sydney • Auckland • New York • Toronto • London • Mexico City • New Delhi
Hong Kong • Buenos Aires • Puerto Rico

ISBN 978-1-76152-651-0

Printed in China.

MIX
Paper | Supporting responsible forestry
FSC® C023121

This product is made of material from well-managed FSC®-certified forests, recycled materials, and other controlled sources.

JURASSIC WORLD

CHAOS THEORY

Volume One
The Novelisation

Adapted by Steve Behling
Cover illustrated by Patrick Spaziante

SCHOLASTIC
SYDNEY AUCKLAND NEW YORK TORONTO LONDON MEXICO CITY
NEW DELHI HONG KONG BUENOS AIRES PUERTO RICO

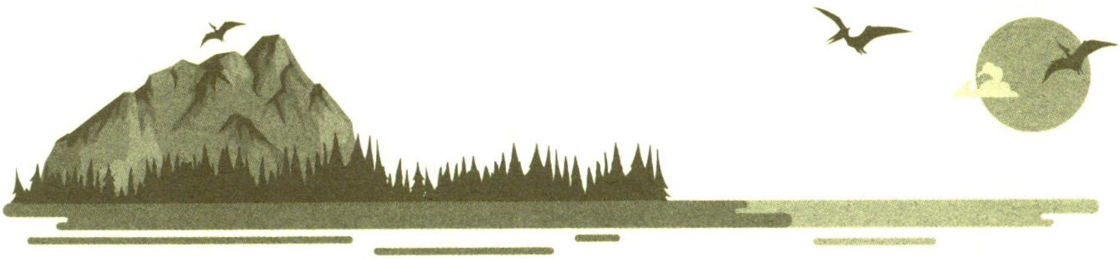

CHAPTER ONE

Eighteen-year-old Darius Bowman flipped through radio stations as he bumped down the rough rural road in his pickup truck.

"And with the six-year anniversary of the fall of Jurassic World fast approaching," a newscaster's voice said, "our minds turn to those heroic teens known as the Nublar Six, especially in the wake of last spring's tragic passing of—"

The newscast was cut short by an alarm blaring over the radio.

"This is not a test," a voice said. "Listeners are advised to stay inside. Dinosaurs have been sighted off Route 693, near mile marker 7. Department of Prehistoric Wildlife officers have been dispatched. Please avoid the area. Repeat, please avoid the area—"

Darius slammed his foot down on the accelerator. "DPW Dispatch, we've got eyes on the prize. He's a big one," Ronnie said into the walkie-talkie. The DPW officer was at mile marker 7 with her partner, Mike, who grabbed a tranquilizer device from their truck.

"Copy that," Dispatch replied. "The relocation team is on the way. Just sit tight, keep your distance, and continue to observe."

Ronnie signed off as she and Mike slowly approached something that was making loud rumbling and equally loud snorting noises.

They heard a loud *SNAP,* and both officers jumped as a few apples rolled toward their feet. Whipping their heads around, they saw an apple tree on its side, the roots sticking out of the ground. Right next to the tree was a four-ton *Pachyrhinosaurus*! The horned dinosaur ignored the officers as it munched on apples.

Ronnie stood still. She looked at her partner, and her eyes went wide when she saw Mike level the tranquilizer device at the *Pachyrhinosaurus.*

"What are you—?!" Ronnie said in a hushed voice. "That's an eight-thousand-pound *Pachyrhinosaurus*! You wanna try hauling it out of here unconscious?"

Mike looked over his shoulder and back toward the road . . . which now seemed quite far away. Then he lowered the device.

"Good answer," Ronnie said. "Now, why don't

you go back to the truck, grab a net launcher, and put the tranq device away before you—"

Suddenly, the dinosaur stomped on the ground, bellowing loudly, as if in pain. In response, Mike accidentally fired the tranq device, launching a dart at the *Pachyrhinosaurus.* The dart pinged off the dinosaur's crest, upsetting the creature even more.

Its attention fixed on Mike, the dinosaur grunted and pawed at the ground like it was about to charge!

"What do we do? What do we do?!" a panicky Mike asked.

"You might wanna start by lowering your voice."

Ronnie and Mike turned as Darius exited his pickup truck. He quietly approached the *Pachyrhinosaurus,* hand outstretched. As he passed Mike, Darius lowered the officer's tranq device.

"Hey there, big fella," Darius said. "Seems like you and the officers here got off on the wrong foot."

The dinosaur responded to the calming tones, and Darius moved closer. The creature raised its foot to stomp on the ground once more. That was when Darius noticed something that shouldn't have been there. Raising the *Pachyrhinosaurus*'s foot gently, he removed a sharp piece of barbed wire. The dinosaur bellowed with relief as Darius gave it an apple, petting the animal on its head.

At first, Darius seemed to regard the dinosaur with affection. Then his expression turned cold.

"We both know you'd end my life in a heartbeat if it suited you, don't we?" Darius said. "It's what you all do."

"Bring it in, kid," Ronnie said as she hugged Darius.

"You two know each other?" a surprised Mike said.

"I used to be his boss," Ronnie said. Breaking the hug, she looked at Darius and said, "If you're *this* desperate to chase dinosaurs, we'd gladly have you back at the DPW."

"Not *all* dinosaurs," Darius said. "Just the one."

Ronnie gave him a worried look. "Darius . . . catching that dinosaur won't . . . it won't bring your friend back. You gotta stop blaming yourself—"

Darius glared at Ronnie.

"Right," Ronnie said, and cleared her throat. "Any leads?"

"Been sightings in this general area," Darius said. "When the alert came over the radio, I thought this might be it." "Officially, I should say leave it to the professionals," Ronnie said. "But . . . just be careful."

It was around then that Darius noticed the *Pachyrhinosaurus* was no longer eating apples. The dinosaur sniffed the air, an alert look on its face. Something was off. Out of the corner of his eye, Darius saw something move.

Before Darius could warn anyone, a snarling *Allosaurus* broke through the trees. The dinosaur's right eye was a sickening milky white, and Darius saw broken crossbow bolts sticking out from the area around it.

Darius dove out of the way of the *Allosaurus,* along with Ronnie and Mike. The dinosaur ran toward the *Pachyrhinosaurus,* trying to bite the *Pachy*'s neck. The horned creature deflected the attack.

As the dinosaurs clashed, a memory played in Darius's mind: *Himself, staring at his phone. A video call. And on the other end of that call, the same* Allosaurus, *bearing down on the person holding the phone. Then the flashing red-and-blue lights of a police car. Darius, rushing toward a DPW officer. He sees something. Something horrible.*

The din of the dinosaur fight brought Darius back. The *Pachyrhinosaurus* slashed the *Allosaurus* with its horns. The angry predator now looked directly at Ronnie, as if changing its mind about who it wanted to attack.

In one swift motion, Darius scooped up a tranq device from the ground and took aim at the *Allosaurus.* Just as he was about to fire, Mike stumbled into him! Darius missed, and the enraged *Allosaurus* took a step toward him. Before he could make another attempt, the sirens of the DPW Relocation Team's vehicle drew near. The *Allosaurus* swiveled its head toward the sirens, then darted off into the brush.

Darius wasn't about to let the creature get away. Tranq device in hand, he raced to his pickup truck and took off in pursuit. Darius spotted the escaping *Allosaurus* running through the foliage. His foot heavy on the accelerator, he closed the gap between himself and the dinosaur. He was sure that this time, the *Allosaurus* would be his. And maybe it would have been, if the pickup truck hadn't hit a massive pothole in the road—a huge *Apatosaurus* footprint.

WHUNK! Darius lost control of the vehicle as a tire went flat. He succeeded in slowing down, skidding to a halt. The *Allosaurus* disappeared into the woods.

Ronnie offered to help Darius change the tire, but he didn't want help. He wanted the *Allosaurus.* He wanted it to pay for what it had done.

Climbing into their vehicle, Ronnie and Mike followed the DPW Relocation Team as they drove off.

"He's been through a lot," Ronnie said.

"Ya think?" Mike replied. "I can't imagine being abandoned with some kids on a dinosaur-infested island and fighting to survive every day for nearly a year."

"I'm not talking about that," Ronnie said. "I'm talking about what happened *after*."

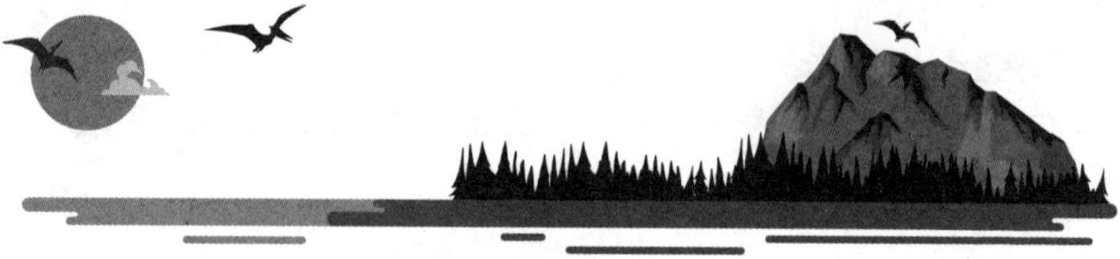

CHAPTER TWO

"You've reached Brooklynn's phone. No one leaves messages anymore . . . just text me! Bye!"

"Hey, it's me," Darius said, sitting in his truck. He looked at a beat-up photo taped to the windshield. Taken just a couple of years ago, the photo showed Darius in his DPW intern uniform, standing with his friends Ben, Kenji, Brooklynn, Sammy, and Yasmina. The Nublar Six.

"I saw it again," Darius continued, leaving the message. "The *Allosaurus.* Almost got it. Don't worry. It won't get away next time. I'll be ready."

He hung up the phone as he arrived at his cabin. Well, technically, it was his family's cabin. Moving past a makeshift wire fence, Darius took note of the various bottles and cans he had attached to it—a crude alarm system. He parked the pickup and retrieved a box from the back of the truck.

Darius opened the gate, clanking the bottles loudly, and went inside the cabin.

The cabin was comfy. Nothing fancy—just a sofa, a small stove, a TV. Pictures hanging on the wall—his mom; his brother, Brand; and Kenji. Darius walked to the kitchen and saw that he had messages on his answering machine.

One was from a reporter with the *NorCal Daily News*. She wanted Darius to "elaborate on his anti-dinosaur sentiments" he had shared right after he left the DPW. The next message was from someone at the DPW who wanted him to come back to work. And the third message was from . . . his brother. A message reminding him that it wouldn't hurt to call his family every once in a while . . . especially his mom.

Darius fiddled with a handheld net launcher while he listened. Then he looked at the screen of an open laptop, and on it, a map, tracking the *Allosaurus*'s path.

By the time Darius had finished fixing the flat tire on his pickup, it was too late to continue the hunt for the *Allosaurus.* He set his phone alarm for five a.m. and headed back inside the cabin for some much-neede sleep. But sleep didn't come, not right away. Restless, Darius sat on the sofa with his laptop and watched a video. It was from six months ago and showed him setting up his "dinosaur alert" fence around the cabin. With him in the video was Brooklynn.

After a while, he picked up the phone and called her.

Voicemail.

"Hiya," Darius began. "I was watching a video and . . . just thought I'd call, but . . . you're not there. Okay. Bye."

Then, and only then, did Darius finally drift off to sleep.

It was 2:47 a.m. when Darius woke up with a start. He couldn't be sure if it was the bad dream that had rudely awakened him or the ring of the landline. Reaching out, Darius grabbed the phone.

No one answered. Then the line went dead.

Outside, he heard the clanging of bottles. His fence alarm! He picked up the stun prod and turned it on.

Something bumped against the front door. Darius closed his eyes, took a deep breath, opened the door,and shoved the stun prod toward a figure in the shadows.

"Darius! You *are* home!"

"Ben?!" Darius said in disbelief. He turned off the stun prod and threw it next to the door. "Ben, I— What are you doing here?!"

Darius looked at his friend. How long had it been since they had seen each other? And how had Ben gotten so tall? He had to be over six feet now!

Ben made small talk as they headed inside the cabin. But Darius could tell that his friend was stalling. There was something on Ben's mind. Why else would he have shown up in the middle of the night?

Rubbing his hands together nervously, Ben said, "That night . . . that awful night that . . . the *Allosaurus* . . ."

"The *Allosaurus*!" Darius exclaimed. "That's what this is about! You're tracking the *Allosaurus,* too!"

"What?" Ben said, sounding confused.

Darius told Ben how he had seen the *Allosaurus,* and that he planned to find it in the morning.

"I almost had it," Darius said. "I was so close. I even called Brooklynn to tell her that—"

"Wait, what? Brooklynn?" Ben asked.

Darius paused awkwardly.

"Darius . . . Brooklynn's dead," Ben said.

Darius didn't know what to say. *Of course* he knew that Brooklynn was dead. But her father had never turned off her voicemail, and Darius explained to Ben that sometimes, he called her number just to hear her voice. To talk about what was going on in his life. To say . . . sorry.

"Darius . . . it wasn't your fault," Ben said.

"We both know that isn't true, Ben," Darius replied. "If I had met her that night like I said I would, then she might—"

"No," Ben said. "That's why I'm here. It wouldn't have mattered. Brooklynn's death was no accident. She was targeted. That *Allosaurus*—"

"—is a wild animal, Ben. A mindless killer. You think it had a grudge against her or something? It was a random dinosaur attack. Happens way too often these days."

"It wasn't random! There's too much coincidence! What was Brooklynn even doing there that night? She never told you, did she? And how did she and the *Allosaurus* end up at the same place at the same time? How did the DPW truck respond so quickly? Why wasn't her phone recovered from the scene? Something's off. I've been reading some stuff on Dark Jurassic, and—"

Darius crossed his arms. "Dark Jurassic? That website where all those bizarros share their weird dinosaur conspiracy theories?"

Looking at the laptop on Darius's coffee table, Ben went to the keyboard and logged into the Dark Jurassic site. He explained that he had been reading about *Allosaurus* migration and had checked out the leaked dinosaur attack photos.

"All of a sudden, someone anonymously starts asking me if I was a member of the Nublar Six," Ben said. "I figured it was a goof, but then I started getting DMs, *hostile* DMs, asking why I was so interested in the night Brooklynn died. Look!"

He tried to show his mailbox to Darius, but the folder was completely empty.

"What? They're . . . not here. Someone must've deleted them. But how—?" Ben said.

"Look, Ben," Darius said gently. "It's been tough on all of us since we got back to the mainland, finding our place back in society, and then Brooklynn . . ."

"Whoever killed Brooklynn is coming after the rest of us, too!" Ben said. "You, me, Yaz, Sammy, Kenji. We're all in danger. And we have to find out why, and who's after us, before it's too late!"

"So you show up here, crank call me, then go on and on about—"

"I didn't crank call you," Ben said. "I didn't call you at all."

Sensing something, Darius shut off the lights. He put a finger to his lips, pointing toward a window in the kitchen.

There, illuminated by the moon, was the unmistakable shadow of a *Velociraptor*.

"Why didn't your fence alarm go off?" Ben whispered. "I closed the gate behind me."

Before Darius could answer, he saw the alarmed look on Ben's face. The shadow of another *Velociraptor* fell against the living room blinds.

Darius thought he heard a high-pitched whistle, and then the two dinosaurs crashed through the windows, invading the cabin! The predators blocked the exits. Darius and Ben were trapped!

Diving for the stun prod by the door, Darius rolled out of the way of a charging *Velociraptor*. The dinosaur slammed into a bookcase, which fell over, trapping the creature.

Across the room, the other *Velociraptor* came for Ben, who grabbed the kitchen table to use as a shield. The dinosaur's head smashed through the table, its jaws trying to chomp down on Ben!

With the stun prod in his hand, Darius glanced across the room and saw the net launcher. He looked at Ben, catching his eye. All that time they had spent being chased by dinosaurs on Isla Nublar and Mantah Corp. Island had taught the two friends that they could survive anything if they worked together.

Darius threw the stun prod to Ben and dove for the net launcher, just as the *Velociraptor* freed itself from the bookcase.

Ben caught the stun prod, zapping the *Velociraptor* before it could reach him through the table!

Darius fired the net, knocking the dinosaur that was coming after him to the ground.

The duo ran out the door, leaving the *Velociraptors* behind.

Or so they thought.

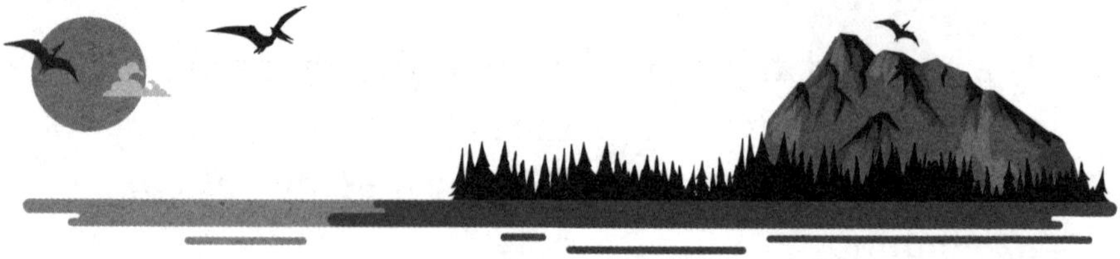

CHAPTER THREE

"Aw, crud," Darius said.

Standing in the darkness was a white *Velociraptor.* It sprinted toward them, gaining speed. Darius and Ben heard a high-pitched whistle in the distance as the dinosaur bore down on them.

Just as the *Velociraptor* pounced, Darius dove to the left, and Ben to the right. They went over the porch railing as the dinosaur collided with the cabin door!

But the creature wasn't down for the count. Back on its feet, the *Velociraptor* resumed the chase. Ben and Darius ran for Darius's truck. Unfortunately for Darius, he tripped on something and fell to the ground. There, he saw scattered bottles and cans from his alarm system.

"What the—??" he began, until a soul-searing screech from the *Velociraptor* interrupted him.

Rushing to his feet, Darius bolted for the pickup. He dove in, and Ben followed. Then there were two slams—Ben shutting the door, and the *Velociraptor* bashing into it.

Darius was just about to start the truck when he realized—the keys were in the cabin! The other *Velociraptors* burst out of the cabin as the white dinosaur collided with the pickup truck again.

As the predator circled the truck, Ben pointed through the windshield.

"My van's just down that way!" he said urgently.

Darius squinted and saw a van parked deep in some trees.

"Why'd you park so far away?!" he demanded.

"I was afraid I was being followed!" Ben explained.

The white *Velociraptor* slammed into the truck again. The vehicle wobbled, and Darius glanced down at the gearshift.

"Glad I changed the tire," Darius said. He shifted the truck into neutral just as the *Velociraptor* rammed into it. The pickup moved forward—and because Darius had put the vehicle in neutral, it rolled down the road, toward Ben's van.

The truck gathered steam as it rolled, and it looked like the boys had lost the *Velociraptor* . . . until they heard a loud thud and felt something land in the bed of the pickup! A dinosaur clawed at the rear window.

Thinking fast, Ben ordered Darius to hit the brakes and turn left on his mark. The truck skidded along the dirt. The *Velociraptor* lost its footing, sailed over the side of the truck, and hit the ground.

Darius and Ben jumped out of the still-moving pickup, rolled on the ground, and ran to the van. They made it inside as another raptor jumped at them. Darius zapped it with the stun prod, and the dazed dinosaur collapsed.

Ben took the wheel and they headed down the road, away from Darius's cabin. In a side-view mirror, Darius could see they had company—the two *Velociraptors* that had invaded the cabin were now chasing the van!

Darius clutched the grab handle above the window as Ben turned the wheel hard to the right. They took a tight turn on a sharp curve just as one of the *Velociraptors* launched itself at the van. The creature slammed into the side, bounced off, and rolled down the side of the mountain. The van swerved and almost went off the road.

They had lost one of the dinosaurs, but the other was still right behind them. Darius wondered why the predators were still following them. If they wanted food, wasn't there an easier way to get it?There was another sharp curve coming, and then another. Ben pushed the van faster and faster, making the turns as tight as possible.

Looking back, Darius couldn't see the second *Velociraptor.*

"I think we lost—" he started, just as the dinosaur's head appeared next to Ben's window!

The creature dug its claws into the van, desperate to get inside. Ahead, Ben saw a slight opening in the trees to one side. Without warning, Ben jerked the steering wheel, and the van careened off the road and through the gap. They headed down the rough, uneven terrain, with no sign of any dinosaurs anywhere.

Once they were back on the road, Darius tried to make sense of what had just happened: the *Velociraptor* attack at the cabin, the dismantled alarm system, the predators pursuing the van, all of it.

There was something about the *Velociraptors* that bothered him. They looked almost like *Atrociraptors*! But Darius thought the only place those dinosaurs had been spotted was at the Lockwood Estate, where dinosaur hybrids had been sold to the highest bidder.

While Darius could almost accept that the *Atrociraptors* showing up at his cabin at the same moment as Ben was a coincidence, the fact that his alarm system appeared to have been sabotaged made him think otherwise.

"I'm telling you, someone is after us," Ben said.

"But why? And who would even want to do that?" Darius asked. "Who would want to . . . hunt us?"

Ben said that he had some theories and directed Darius to the back of his van.

Sliding a door, Darius slipped into the back, where he saw Ben's setup. Along with string lights, speakers, and a microwave, there were a ton of sticky notes on the van's sides. He saw one note stuck to a table that folded into the wall. Moving the table into the open position, he saw a conspiracy theory board, with various points of interest connected by strands of yarn, photos, and even more sticky notes.

" 'Carnivorous locusts'?" Darius read aloud. " 'Big Shaving Cream behind it all'? Ben, what the heck are these?"

"They're theories!" Ben said. Some were his own;some were from that Dark Jurassic website. But, Ben noted, it didn't matter *who* was chasing them at the moment. Only that someone *was* chasing them.

"We're *all* in danger," Ben said. "We gotta warn everyone."

"Fine," Darius said. "I'll call Sammy."

He took out his phone, but before he could make the call, Ben snatched the phone from his hand and threw it out his window.

"What are you doing?!" Darius said. That was the phone . . . that was the phone he used to call Brooklynn!

"Phones are traceable," Ben offered. "They're not safe!"

There would be no phone calls to Sammy, Yaz, or Kenji. It was in person or nothing.

So Ben and Darius were taking a road trip to warn Sammy . . . in Texas.

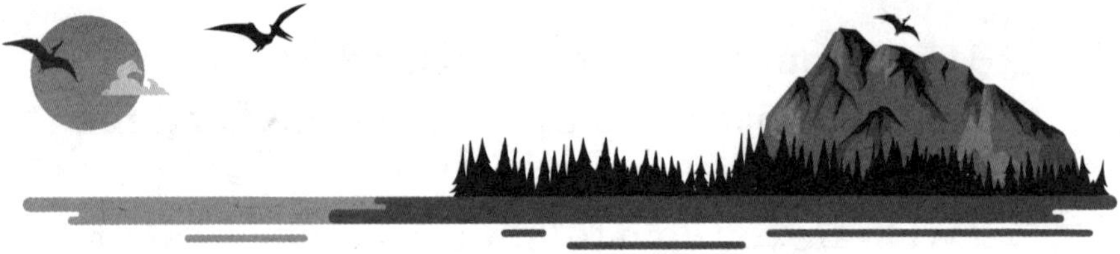

CHAPTER FOUR

How many hours had they been on the road? How many bags of chips had they eaten? Darius had lost count. For a while there, Darius thought maybe they were being followed by a sedan. But it was probably just his imagination.

All he knew was that it was daytime when the van he and Ben had been traveling in finally rolled up on a small cattle ranch.

Ben parked and hopped out of the van along with Darius. Both looked back at the road and beyond, searching for any signs that they might have been followed.

“We get in, tell Sammy what’s up, get her to come with us, and get out,” Ben said.

“Let’s just make it quick so we can get back on the road,” Darius said.

“So you *do* believe me?”

"I wouldn't go that far, but . . . it can't hurt to be too careful."

Approaching the house, the boys caught a whiff of something that smelled . . . not great.

"Is that the hay?" Darius said, waving his hand in front of his nose. "It is *strong.*"

"Must be Biosyn hay," Ben replied. "Word is the stuff notoriously reeks. But it's not just that. Do you also smell—"

"Smoke!" Darius shouted.

A steady stream of smoke poured out the front door, and the boys covered their mouths and ran inside. Had someone gotten to Sammy before they did?

Inside, Ben and Darius shouted Sammy's name.

From the smoke stepped Sammy, a streak of red in her hair. She had an oven mitt on one hand and carried a large hay fork in the other. Sammy beamed at the sight of her old friends.

"Oh my goodness! Darius! Ben!" she said, squeezing them in one of her patented bear hugs. "Sorry about the smoke! Burnt my pie, but the backup's already in the oven! Always have a backup!"

Setting the hay fork down, Sammy walked back toward the kitchen as the smoke cleared.

"Come in, come in! Welcome to my home. She's a bit of a mess right now, but I wasn't expecting guests or anything like that!"

As she walked, Sammy stepped on a floorboard that let out a loud creak. "Woop! Keep meanin' to fix that."

She led her friends to the kitchen and immediately offered them each a glass of lemonade. Something about the frenzied pace, and the way that Sammy seemed to constantly be in motion, talking, had Darius worried. Something wasn't right, but he couldn't put his finger on it.

Sammy took a quick sip of her own lemonade, and Ben decided that was the perfect time to tell her what was going on.

"Sammy, we're here because we're—"

BEEP! A kitchen timer cut Ben off, and Sammy jumped up.

"That'll be the backup pie!" Sammy said. She flew to the oven, looked in the window, and said, "Not there yet!"

A little more forcefully, Ben said, "Sammy, we're here to warn—"

"Oh, Sammy, ya ding-dong! Of course you'd want to go out back first!" she said, slapping her forehead as if she'd made the hugest mistake.

Then she grabbed Ben by the hand and pulled him outside. Sammy guided Ben toward a large horse shelter as Darius trailed behind.

"You nervous about seeing her?" Sammy asked.

"See her? *Now?*" Ben practically stammered.

"Wait, what are we talking about?" Darius said, completely clueless.

"Dang it!" Sammy cursed. "Not again!"

Darius saw a wooden fence that divided Sammy's ranch and the property next door. It looked like a horse . . . or maybe something much bigger than a horse . . . had trampled it.

Sammy took off in the direction of the downed fence, with Ben and Darius right behind her.

"Why are we running?!" Darius said. "We do not have a good track record with *running*!"

As he ran past the broken fence, Darius felt more confused than ever. Why were they running? What were they running after?

Then he looked up ahead, and all at once, Darius had his answers. There in a pasture, happily munching on mouthfuls of grass, was an *Ankylosaurus.*

"Bumpy?!" Darius said in disbelief.

The dinosaur bellowed with joy as it chased birds through a field. Whatever anxiety Ben may have been feeling seemed to fall away as he ran toward his old friend."Bumper Car!" Ben called out. Recognizing the voice, Bumpy galloped right toward him. She slowed as she approached Ben, then tilted her head down. Very gently, she lifted him just off the ground, nuzzling him.

"We snuck her out right before the whole Mantah Corp. Island investigation," Sammy said.

While Ben got reacquainted with Bumpy, Darius thought he would catch up with Sammy.

"How's Yaz?" he asked.

"Good! I think," Sammy answered.

"You think? You mean you . . . ?" Then Darius made a motion with his hands, as if breaking something.

"No! Nothin' like that," Sammy said. "You knew she was up north finishing her psych program, right? We've been doing the long-distance thing awhile now, and it's . . . not easy. I sure do miss her, and wish she'd answer her phone more. But we're all busy. You know how it is!"

Darius nodded, only too aware of how easy it was to get caught up in oneself.

"Do your parents still do all this, ya know, farm stuff, too?"

Sammy's mood seemed to take a turn as she said, "They still got their cattle ranch. We had a bit of a falling-out about it, actually. But that ain't bringing me down!"

Darius felt terrible, like he'd been the worst friend. "I'm sorry, Sammy, that—"

Before he could finish, Sammy let out an earsplitting "HIYA!" and released a roundhouse kick at Darius's face! He barely managed to duck out of the way.

"Did I mention I'm also really into capoeira now?" Sammy said.

"I think you just did!" Darius said, dusting himself off. "Sammy, if you need someone to talk to about everything going on—"

But Sammy wasn't listening. She was heading toward Ben and Bumpy as she said, "I love seeing friends reunite, probs more than anyone, but we *really* need to get outta here before—"

Interrupted by a noisy engine, Sammy and the others turned to see dirt and smoke kicked up from the ground as a truck approached.

"Too late!" Sammy said.

The tires squealed as the truck came at them. It showed no signs of slowing down!

"Get out of the way!" Sammy yelled.

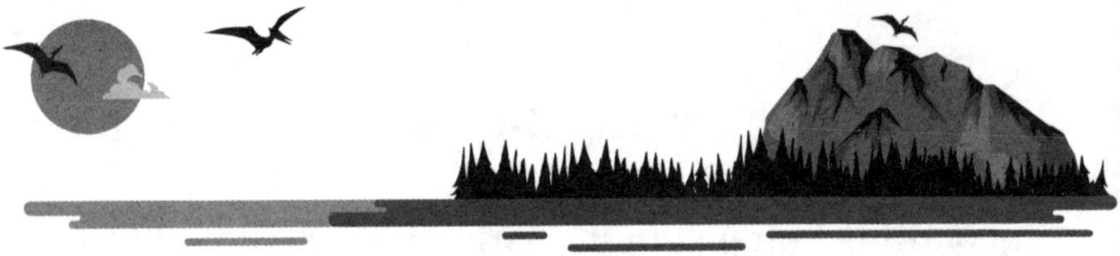

CHAPTER FIVE

Sammy, Ben, and Darius dove out of the way of the oncoming truck and were surprised when it kept going—it wasn't coming for them.

It was coming for Bumpy!

The dinosaur bellowed, shifting her body just in time to smack the truck with her tail. The driver jumped out of the vehicle right before it flipped onto its side.

"Carl, are you okay?" Sammy asked, rushing over to the driver.

"See that?!" Carl said, standing up. "It's trying to kill me!"

The older man shot Bumpy a mean look.

"To be fair, you *did* try to run her down with your truck," Sammy offered.

But Carl wasn't in the mood to listen to reason. He went on and on about Bumpy being a "destructive carnivore," ranting about how the *Ankylosaurus* had been eating his crops.

"I just can't wait to call the DPW and see that creature dragged outta here," Carl fumed. "There's *nothing* you can say to defend that monster this time."

Ben had heard enough and walked to Carl. Towering over the man, Ben said, "*She's* not the monster here."

Sammy tried to defuse the situation. "Now, let's all hold our horses a moment and not do anything more to escalate this predicament than we already have."

After a while, Sammy was able to send Carl on his way with the promise of mending the fence and bringing him a freshly baked pie. Carl trudged back to his house in silence while Sammy led Bumpy to her stall.

It was dark outside as Sammy raced into her kitchen. Darius and Ben lagged behind, trying to keep up with her frantic pace.

"Darius and I need to talk to you," Ben said gravely.

Sammy whirled around with the pie in her hand,clocking the serious looks on both boys' faces.

This was not going to be good.

"Someone is hunting us," Ben continued. "I don't know who, but I think those same people were behind Brooklynn's death—and they're after all of us. That means we need to warn Yaz and Kenji."

"Yaz and Kenji are in trouble?" Sammy said.

"Yes. If these people—and raptors, apparently—find any of us, they'll . . . it won't be good. Which means finding the others before they do," Ben said.

"Then we gotta warn them," Sammy said, setting the pie on the kitchen table.

Sammy hurried down the hallway, past the open door of her guest room. She couldn't help looking inside. A pink jacket hung over the back of a chair.

It was Brooklynn's jacket.

She had asked Sammy to keep it for her after her last visit.

Lost in thought, Sammy almost didn't notice Ben and Darius staring at her.

Snapping out of it, she said, "Just gotta get some supplies for our trip."

Sammy dashed into a room and returned with a box of supplies, dumping it into Ben's arms.

"Kenji's place is on the way to Yaz's," she said. "He keeps changing his number, but I can call Yaz while we're on the road. I think there's a map around here somewhere. Service is terrible from here to Wyoming."

"Great. Now can we please get on the road?" Ben begged.

"In a second. I still need to—"

"Sammy, stop!" Darius said. "Please, just . . . stop."

At that moment, all the emotion that had been bottled up inside Sammy burst out. "Stop?! Stop and what, Darius? Stop and think about Brooklynn dying or my family not speaking to me or Yaz pulling away from me? No, I . . . I *can't* stop."

Instantly, Darius felt awful. He was about to say something when they heard Bumpy bellowing outside.

At least, Ben thought it was Bumpy.

Then the lights went out—both inside the house and out.

"I just fixed the breaker box last week," Sammy said. Then, as if she knew the source of the problem, she said, "Carl."

Sammy told Darius and Ben to go check on Bumpy while she fixed the breaker.

As they walked toward Bumpy's stall, Darius thought he heard a faint whistling. Maybe it was the wind? Then they saw something move in the dark, in a field up ahead.

"We know you're out here, Carl!" Ben shouted. "Stop messing with our dinosaur!"

But whatever it was . . . it wasn't Carl. It was

coming closer, and Ben and Darius ducked behind a hay bale for cover.

The white *Atrociraptor* raised its head, sniffing the air, searching.

"The raptors! They found us!" Ben whispered.

"How?" Darius wondered. "We're over a thousand miles from my cabin."

Ben's eyes drifted toward Bumpy's shelter, where he saw another *Atrociraptor* approaching. He knew he had to help Bumpy.

"I'll get Sammy," Darius said. "Meet up at the van after."

Inside the house, Sammy flipped the switch on the breaker box, but no lights came on.

Looking out a window, she saw Darius staring back at her. He glanced behind him, and Sammy's eyes followed . . . landing on an *Atrociraptor.*

Darius pointed toward Ben's van, and Sammy immediately understood. She headed for the hallway but found her path blocked by another *Atrociraptor*! Backing away, she snuck into the guest room, closing the door silently.

Sammy searched the room for anything she could use to defend herself but came up blank. Seeing Brooklynn's jacket, Sammy picked it up and held on to it. Something about it made her feel like everything was going to be okay.

Gently, Sammy set the jacket on the back of the chair, then she saw something fall out of a pocket—a folded piece of paper. She took it as the *Atrociraptor* neared the door.

The *Atrociraptor* was getting closer. Ben ducked into the empty stall right next to Bumpy's. The creature stalked by Bumpy's enclosure and went into the one where Ben was hiding! Catching a scent, the dinosaur pounced.

But Ben wasn't there. He had tricked the *Atrociraptor,* escaping at the last possible second. Slamming the enclosure door shut, Ben trapped the predator!

He opened Bumpy's gate and gave his friend a quick hug before releasing her into the wild.

Darius hated the smell of the hay, but there was nothing he could do about it. The white *Atrociraptor* had been coming for him, so Darius was forced to hide inside a hay shed, where he was now overcome by the obnoxious odor.

The predator entered the shed, searching for Darius. But the smell of the hay masked Darius's scent! Confused, the *Atrociraptor* ran out of the shed, as if it were retracing its steps. At least for the moment, Darius was safe.

Cracking the door of the guest room, Sammy looked toward the kitchen. There, she saw the *Atrociraptor* sniffing the pie on the table. The dinosaur knocked it to the floor with a loud clang, and Sammy took that as a sign to get out of there, now.

Sneaking down the hallway, Sammy carefully stepped around the creaky floorboard. She was almost at the front door when she accidentally knocked over the hay fork!

The *Atrociraptor* jerked its head in her direction and hurtled down the hallway!

Sammy grabbed the fork and spun out the open door. The dinosaur followed as Sammy kicked the door closed on its face! Then she wedged the fork under the doorknob. It wouldn't hold for long, but maybe just long enough.

Dashing for the van, Sammy saw that Ben and Darius were already there. Ben jumped inside the vehicle and started the engine, while Darius got in the back.

"Hurry! Hurry!" Darius shouted to Sammy.

She sprinted toward the van just as the *Atrociraptor* broke out of the house.

Ben put the van in reverse as Darius reached his hand out from the back. Darius couldn't help but think of Brooklynn, and how he hadn't been able to save her. He wasn't about to let that happen again.

But the predator was coming too fast. There was no way Sammy would make it. It would take a miracle . . .

. . . or an *Ankylosaurus.*

From out of nowhere, Bumpy appeared, slamming the snarling carnivore with her tail. The predator went flying as Darius pulled Sammy into the van.

In his side mirror, Ben watched as Bumpy pressed the attack against the *Atrociraptor,* smack ing it with her tail one more time. Now the predator was out of the fight.

"Yes! Atta girl, Bumpy!" Ben shouted, and the van sped off into the night.

Inside the cab, everyone took a deep breath. They were safe, for the moment. There was just one problem: How were they going to find their friends?

Sammy remembered the piece of paper that had fallen out of Brooklynn's jacket. She unfolded the paper to reveal a map, with each of the Nublar Six's addresses marked on it.

Darius smiled as he thought about Brooklynn's resourcefulness. Then he noticed a sticky note on the map. It bore a time and an address.

"That one's Kenji's," Sammy said. "But the one right near it . . . I don't know."

"The date and time she wrote down . . . that's the week before she died," Darius said solemnly.

"If she wasn't going to see Kenji . . . where was she going?" Ben asked.

Back at Sammy's ranch, a hand opened the pen where the *Atrociraptor* had been trapped. Then there came a sharp whistle, and the dinosaur took off, joining up with the other two predators in its pack. They ran over to a large water delivery truck. At least, that was what it said on the side of the truck. But when the doors opened, there were carriers inside—one for each of the three *Atrociraptors.* They jumped inside, and the hand closed the doors.

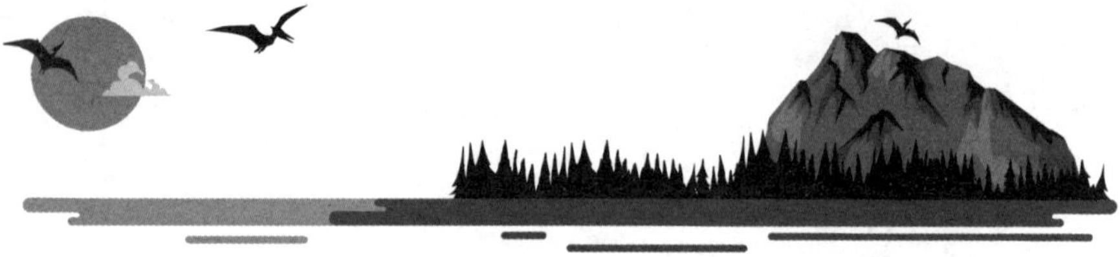

CHAPTER SIX

The van had just crossed the border into Colorado, but something was still bothering Darius. "Those raptors . . . if they're the same ones from my cabin, they would've had to track us over fifteen hundred miles and still gotten to Texas not long after we did," he said.

"Almost makes ya feel like we're being hunted, don't it?" Ben said pointedly from behind the wheel.

"I know it was dark," Darius continued, "but they looked kinda . . . different."

Ben wondered if maybe the *Atrociraptors* had some kind of camouflaging capability, like the Indominus rex.

Peeking out from the back of the van, Sammy said, "Yaz is still not pickin' up her phone."

As Sammy climbed into the seat behindDarius, an exasperated Ben said, "Sammy, how many times do I gotta tell you? Cellphones are traceable!"

"You'd do the same thing if you had a girlfriend," Sammy said.

"I definitely wouldn't, because I do, and I haven't," Ben replied.

Both Sammy and Darius were surprised by Ben's admission that he had a girlfriend. They were even more surprised when Ben said she lived in Italy.

From behind the van, an air horn startled Ben. Sirens followed as he pulled to the side of the highway. A DPW caravan passed, hauling captured dinosaurs in their rigs. Darius spotted a *Baryonyx,* a *Carnotaurus,* and even a *Sinoceratops* among them.

And then, in the very last truck, Darius saw something that made his stomach turn. There was the *Allosaurus*—the same one he had been after. He couldn't take his eyes off it.

After several more hours of driving, the van arrived at a beat-up trailer parked near some tall pine trees. In the background, mountains loomed.

"This . . . is Kenji's place?" Darius asked as the friends climbed out of the van.

"I knew his dad lost all their money when Mantah Corp. went under and he went to prison . . . ," Ben said.

"When we *sent* him to prison," Sammy corrected him.

". . . but I wasn't expecting this," Ben finished.

Ben knocked on the trailer door, but there was no answer.

"Hmmm . . . you sure this is the right address?" Ben asked.

Sammy knocked as a voice behind them said, "Maybe try knocking one more time?"

The voice startled the three friends. Sammy spun around and gave a capoeira kick, hitting a man in his stomach. The man doubled over, and it was then that Sammy saw him drop a rope and a backpack.

It was Kenji!

"Good to see you . . . too," Kenji groaned from the ground.

"Kenji?? Oh my goodness, don't sneak up on us like that!" Sammy said.

"Not sneaking," Kenji said, winded. "Just coming home from teaching rock climbing."

Ben helped Kenji to his feet as the rock climber said, "Dude! You've gotten tall!"

Then Kenji gave Sammy a hug before approaching Darius.

"Hey . . . Kenj," Darius said slowly. "I know last time I saw you . . . it wasn't great, but—"

As if he hadn't heard a word Darius said, Kenji

headed toward the trailer door. He unlocked it and motioned for Sammy and Ben to come inside. When Darius tried to enter, Kenji let the door close behind him.

Gritting his teeth, Darius opened the door and entered.

"Welcome to Casa de Kenji two point oh!" Kenji said.

The trailer itself was sparse. There was a mattress on the floor, a mini-fridge, and lots and lots of cardboard boxes, all of which were labeled BUMPER STICKERS. Darius could see that the bumper stickers advertised Kenji's rock-climbing business.

Looking around, Darius saw a picture frame beneath a stack of stickers. He picked it up and saw a photo that he immediately recognized as having been taken in his own cabin. There was Darius's mom; his brother, Brand; Kenji; and . . . someone who was covered by a sticky note with a grocery list written on it.

Darius lifted the sticky and saw his own face.

He almost wanted to say "What gives?" to Kenji, when he heard Ben say, "We came to warn you . . . we're all in danger."

Kenji dismissed the idea. "I don't do danger anymore. I'm more of an 'eat, climb, love' kinda guy now."

"Great in theory, until raptors show up at your

door," Sammy said.

"Raptors?" Kenji said, his interest piqued. "For real?"

"Yeah, for real," Darius said, still holding the photo. "Why do you think we're here? It's definitely not for the sparkling conversation."

For a moment, Darius locked eyes with Kenji.

"Brooklynn's death," Ben said, "wasn't an accident."

This clearly struck a nerve with Kenji. "What—? No, you . . . you don't know what you're talking about."

"The *Allosaurus,* that night . . . Brooklynn was targeted," Ben insisted.

Kenji shook his head, then gave Darius a look that could kill.

"*Someone's* to blame for her death, but it's not a bunch of dinosaurs," Kenji said.

"We don't know what's going on," Sammy said. "But we do know someone's using dinos to come after *us.* Brooklynn's death . . . well, things don't add up. I found this map she left, with a note—"

Sammy gestured to Darius, who pulled the map from his pocket and gave it to her. She showed the map to Kenji, pointing out an address that wasn't far from Kenji's trailer.

"The note's dated a week before she . . . you know," Sammy said.

Darius noted the look on Kenji's face when he read the address. It was like he had seen the living dead.

Kenji said that he had never been to that address before.

It was where his father lived.

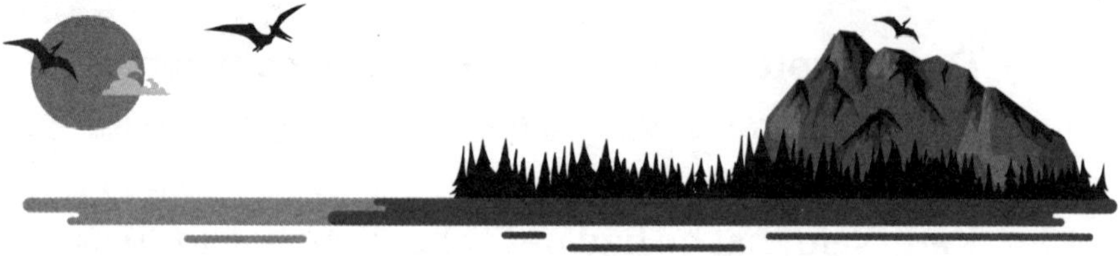

CHAPTER SEVEN

Ben stared at Kenji, trying to wrap his brain around what he'd learned. Had Brooklynn *really* met with Kenji's dad—the person who tried to leave them for dead on a dinosaur-filled island—just before she . . . well, just before?

Suddenly, the trailer began to shake.

"Whoa . . . what is that?" Ben wondered.

"Did those raptors catch up to us?!" Sammy said as boxes of bumper stickers fell to the floor around them.

Steadying themselves against the walls of the trailer, Darius, Ben, and Sammy looked at their host. Kenji appeared almost calm as a framed rock-climbing poster fell toward the floor. Kenji caught the frame.

"They'll be done in a minute," he said.

Peering through the blinds, Darius saw a herd

of *Parasaurolophuses* stampeding past the trailer. They ran into each other but somehow managed to avoid Kenji's home. Until they didn't, and a *Parasaurolophus* smashed into the trailer's metal siding.

"These *Parasaurolophuses* cross through here every afternoon," Kenji explained. "They nest in the valley down the trail."

The shaking stopped, and Sammy said, "I'm gonna go try Yaz again."

She went outside, leaving Darius with Ben and Kenji.

"Why would Brooklynn go see my dad the week before she died?" Kenji said.

Ben suggested that Kenji's dad was involved with Brooklynn's death.

Kenji dismissed the idea. His dad had been in a halfway house since getting out of prison. The place was monitored 24/7. Even if he had wanted to, Kenji's dad wouldn't have been able to do anything.

"He and Brooklynn talked about something," Ben said. "We should go see him."

"What?! No! No way," Kenji protested. "I am *not* talking to that man. We are done . . . forever."

"But what if he knows something that could help us?" Ben said.

"*I'm not going.* I'm in a really good place now. And I got here *by myself.* I'm not about to throw that away for him . . . or anyone else."

Kenji left the trailer, slamming the door behind him. The framed poster that he had saved fell to the floor, the glass shattering.

Darius and Ben went after Kenji as he headed through a stand of trees toward the mountain.

"Where's he going?" Sammy said.

"He didn't exactly take the news about his dad so well," Ben replied.

Pacing back and forth, Sammy said, "Okay, well, Yaz still isn't answering my calls. I know she doesn't *always* answer, but she at least texts back or maybe just gives a thumbs-up. I got that girlfriend intuition that something ain't right."

Then she stopped pacing and said, "I think we should split up."

For a moment, Ben thought Sammy meant that she and Yaz should break up. But Sammy explained that Yaz needed her, and that she was going to see her. Now.

She walked toward Ben, looking like she might kick him. But she didn't. In fact, she did something worse.

She tickled him.

"No! Please!" Ben pleaded, laughing.

"Gimme the keys!" Sammy ordered.

"No, you can't!"

The keys fell out of Ben's pocket, and Sammy scooped them up, heading toward the van.

"Hey! You can't take my van!" he shouted.

Sammy didn't turn back.

"Okay, maybe you can, but I'm coming with you!"

Sammy hopped in the van, getting behind the wheel, as Ben opened the passenger door.

The last thing Darius wanted to do was stick around with Kenji, so he tried to get into the van, too. Except the door was locked, and Ben wouldn't open it.

"Sorry, D. You gotta stay," Ben said. He told Darius that if someone was hunting them, then they needed to have each other's backs. That meant Darius staying with Kenji.

Besides, Sammy pointed out, this might be good for them. Maybe Darius could even convince Kenji to go talk to his dad.

It didn't seem to matter what Darius said—it was apparent that Sammy and Ben were going to get Yaz, and Darius would be staying behind.

Later, when Darius hiked to the base of the mountain, Kenji was already in full climbing gear, scaling the rocky wall. On the ground was a second harness and some ropes just waiting for him.

Darius put on the gear, grabbed the ropes, and

started to climb.

"I thought you didn't do danger anymore!" Darius called up to Kenji. He reached for a rock to pull himself up, but he slipped! He managed to grasp another rock, but then he felt himself losing his footing.

Kenji rappelled down the cliff, almost sighing as he lowered himself next to Darius.

"Thanks, man, I—" Darius started to say, and then Kenji took hold of Darius's rope, causing him to dangle off the side of the mountain.

Glaring at Darius, Kenji said, "Where were you the night Brooklynn died?"

"You wanna talk about this now?!" Darius said, freaking out a little.

"You said you'd be there, and you weren't. *Where were you?* What was so important you'd abandon her like that?"

"Where were *you,* Kenji? You weren't there for her, either. You were her *boyfriend,* but then you—"

That was enough for Kenji. He let go. Darius screamed as he fell . . . just barely. In fact, thanks to his safety equipment, he hardly fell at all.

"That's how climbing ropes work," Kenji said, continuing up the cliff, leaving Darius behind.

When he reached the top of the mountain, Kenji embraced the view. A herd of *Parasaurolophuses* stampeded through the valley below as the sun began to fall behind the rim of mountains in the distance.

He remembered sitting in this same spot, not too long ago, with Brooklynn. He had wanted so much to share the beauty of this place with her. But Brooklynn seemed more interested in her phone and whatever it was she was doing.

It kept happening over and over. Maybe he and Brooklynn were just too different.

Maybe that was why, in that particular moment, Kenji had told Brooklynn that he couldn't be with her anymore.

"Phew!" Darius said, snapping Kenji out of it. "That was . . . way harder than it looks."

Kenji wiped tears from his eyes as Darius approached him.

Taking in the view of the dinosaurs below, Darius said, "Whooaaa. This is *incredible.*"

That actually made Kenji smile. "Of course *you'd* think it's cool."

"Kenji . . . Brooklynn felt bad," Darius said. "After you broke up. For not paying attention. For not appreciating . . . all this."

"How do you know that?" Kenji asked.

"Um, she came and stayed at my cabin with me

for a while," Darius said. "She needed someone to talk to, I guess."

"*She* needed someone," Kenji repeated bitterly.

"I thought you knew," Darius said.

"No, I didn't know," Kenji said, anger rising in his voice. "I didn't know she stayed with you. I didn't know she visited my dad. No one tells me anything."

Then he stood up and bumped into Darius's shoulder on his way to put on his harness.

"We'll go see my dad first thing in the morning."

"Wait, for real?" Darius said, shocked.

Kenji already had his harness on and was just about to go back down when he turned to face Darius.

"Worth a shot," he said. "Someone's gotta be honest with me, right?"

Darius watched as Kenji disappeared over the side of the mountain. He felt awful. When did everything get so complicated?

As the sun went down and the darkness came, Darius heard a twig snapping. He whipped his head around but saw nothing.

Unnerved, he went back down the mountain.

In a forest, alone, Bumpy slumbered beneath a canopy of trees. She was unaware of the truck coming closer, the headlights illuminating the *Ankylosaurus.* Even the sounds of the truck braking and the door opening didn't cause the dinosaur to awaken.

It was only when a foot stepped on some leaves, making a loud crunching sound, that Bumpy at last opened her eyes. She looked left and right, anxious.

Turning her head when she heard more footsteps, Bumpy bleated in alarm . . .

. . . until something made her stop abruptly.

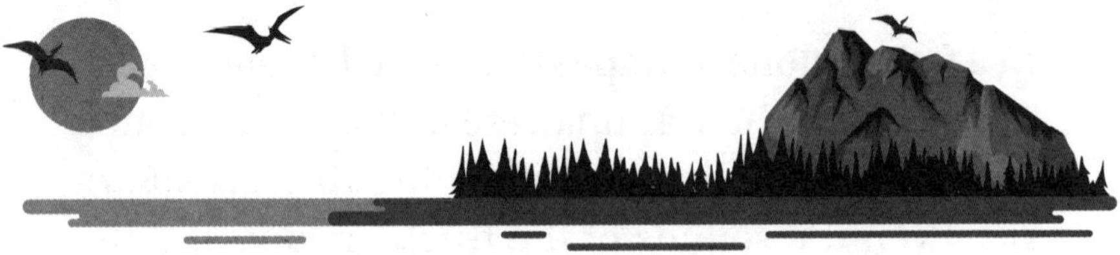

CHAPTER EIGHT

On the ride to the halfway house to visit Kenji's dad, Darius tried to talk with Kenji. But Kenji offered nothing but curt replies. Maybe it was too soon to try to rekindle their friendship, Darius thought.

Kenji pulled his car up to a plain-looking building with a huge garden near a forest. Security cameras seemed to be everywhere, keeping track of their every move. A guard approached Kenji.

"Phones," the guard said flatly. "No outside means of communication on the premises."

Kenji handed his phone to the guard, who then looked at Darius as if to say ". . . and *yours*?"

"No phone," Darius said. "My friend threw it out the window."

Kenji headed down the driveway and parked in front of the house. Staring out the windshield, he let the scene wash over him like a wave. His hands grasped the steering wheel tightly, until at last, he released his grip and said, "Let's go."

They left the car and headed inside with the guard, who escorted them to the garden, where Kenji's father, Daniel Kon, pruned a plant. He wasn't wearing an expensive suit—just plain work clothes and an ankle monitor.

"Mr. Kon, you've got guests," the guard said.

Darius could have sworn he caught a trace of a smile on Mr. Kon's face when the man saw Kenji, but it vanished quickly.

The guard then left, telling Kenji that he could pick up his phone on the way out.

Mr. Kon came to shake his son's hand, but Kenji didn't respond in kind. Instead, he just looked at his father's ankle monitor.

"Nice bling," Kenji said.

"Seems redundant, to be honest," Mr. Kon said. "Surely the guard would stop me before I was able to trip the alarm. Not that I have any intention of running."

The father regarded the son for a moment, then said, "You look good."

Kenji didn't say anything. Darius tried to make small talk about the garden flowers, until Kenji suddenly blurted out, "Did you have Brooklynn killed?"

"I was just as shocked to hear about Brooklynn's death as you were, Son," Mr. Kon said. "But you know I've been at this halfway house for nearly a year, yes? I only ask because you don't live far from here and yet this is the first time you're visiting."

"How do you know where I live?" Kenji asked, surprised.

Mr. Kon didn't elaborate. "And then of course I was in prison for five years before that. So no, I didn't kill your girlfriend."

"Then how do you explain her dying within *days* of coming to see you?" Kenji demanded.

Now it was Mr. Kon's turn to be surprised, and he raised an eyebrow.

"Yeah, you're not the only one who knows things," Kenji said.

Trying to defuse the tension, Darius asked why Brooklynn had come to see Mr. Kon.

"I'll tell you," the man said to Kenji. Then, looking at Darius, he said, "But not in front of *him*. This is family business."

"Fine," Kenji said, and walked off with his father, leaving Darius behind.

With nothing else to do, Darius wandered the garden, full of concern for Kenji. Lost in thought, he backed into some bushes, where he heard rustling. Immediately, he was on edge, wondering if maybe it was the *Atrociraptors.* Could they have found him again?

It wasn't *Atrociraptors,* but a small group of

Compsognathuses that scurried from the bushes. Maybe he was just being paranoid, he thought.

As he turned around, Darius heard a voice say, "Who would have thought your old man would have a green thumb?"

It was Mr. Kon! In his wandering, Darius had gotten close enough that he could hear Kenji's conversation. Unseen, he listened in.

"You still haven't answered our questions," Kenji said.

Darius heard Mr. Kon say something in Japanese and Kenji reply, "Don't do the Japanese thing. You know I don't speak it."

"All those tutors, and you still refuse to take pride in our language," Mr. Kon said.

"I *am* proud," Kenji said. "Just never had a father around to practice with."

"I was never around because I was busy building not just businesses, but a *legacy*. For you," Mr. Kon explained. "I've got some things in motion that will bring honor back to our name, our family. And I want you to be part of it."

Kenji protested in no uncertain terms that he wanted nothing to do with it.

But Mr. Kon said he was trying to make peace with Kenji. "You are my son. . . . You still mean the world to me."

When Kenji didn't reply, his father continued,

"You want this to be business, fine. I'm willing to negotiate. When you and your friends took down Mantah Corp., my face was all over the news. 'Disgraced CEO Brought Down by the Famous Nublar Six.' Makes it hard to find investors."

Mr. Kon said that while he might be a disgrace, Kenji was a hero. People trust a hero. People will invest in a hero.

"My offer is this: I'll tell you everything I know about Brooklynn . . . if you join my new company as CEO."

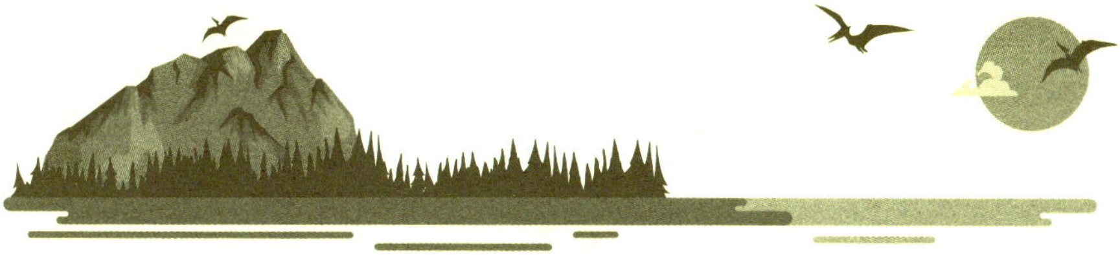

CHAPTER NINE

Darius could only imagine how Kenji must have been feeling. He wasn't surprised when Kenji stormed off, leaving his father behind.

Darius quickly ran after Kenji, who went back to his car.

"Really, Dad? An ultimatum?" Kenji said to himself. " 'You can either sell your soul to me, the literal devil, or never know what was going on with Brooklynn.' "

A moment later, Kenji turned toward Darius and asked, "What would you do?"

Darius couldn't believe Kenji was actually asking for his opinion. He told Kenji that he shouldn't have to make a deal like that, not with a man who was never there for him.

Tears came to Kenji's eyes. "Yeah . . . ," he said slowly, "but if we want to find out why Brooklynn was here, what really happened to her . . . I don't see how I can say no."

"You've returned," Mr. Kon said, pruning another plant. "I take that to mean you agree to my terms?"

"Stop pretending like you gave me a real choice," Kenji said. "Have you ever done anything for anyone else that wasn't for your own selfish gain? Obviously, becoming CEO of whatever shady business you're about to start is my only option."

Mr. Kon smiled as he told Kenji not to worry. He'd be the one doing the actual work. All Kenji would have to do was make a few speeches to the company shareholders. "It'll be easy, Kenji. I know how you like things to be easy."

Through clenched teeth, Kenji said, "'Easy'? What part of this is easy? The part where you left me to die on an island full of dinosaurs? Or maybe forcing me to become your puppet just so I can know the truth? That sounds easy?"

Maybe it was hearing the words said out loud, but something finally clicked with Kenji, and he said, "Ya know what? No. I'm not gonna do it. I won't let you control me anymore. We'll find out about Brooklynn without you. I'm done."

"You're not serious," Mr. Kon said, shocked.

“Keep your secrets. Keep your schemes and ultimatums,” Kenji said. “I don’t need them, and I don’t need you. Goodbye, Dad.”

And then Kenji walked away, Darius following.

With his bluff called, now Mr. Kon was the one with no choice.

“Wait! I’ll . . . I’ll tell you about Brooklynn,” he said as Kenji stopped and looked at him.

“No more tricks?” Kenji asked.

“No more tricks. Just . . . stay?” Mr. Kon asked. “A little longer?”

Kenji took a step toward his father. “She came to see me about dinosaurs being where they shouldn’t, illegally. Buying, selling, the like. Given my past, she thought I had something to do with it. I didn’t.”

“What did you tell her?” Darius asked Mr. Kon.

“It wasn’t so much what I told her as what she told me,” Mr. Kon said. “That she wanted to get in the game. I believe her exact words were ‘I’m not afraid to get my hands dirty.’ ”

“Yeah, right,” Kenji scoffed.

“Look, Son, you don’t want to go down this road. When she came here, there was something about her that was different. Almost . . . dangerous. I just didn’t think she’d be foolish enough to get herself killed.”

That was enough for both Kenji and Darius, and

they moved toward Mr. Kon. But then Darius suddenly turned his head and said, "SHH! Listen."

"I don't hear anything," Kenji replied.

"Exactly," Darius said. It was completely quiet. No animal sounds, nothing. Then the *Compsognathuses* that Darius had seen earlier came out from the trees, running away. The next sound they heard was a high-pitched whistle.

"We have to go," Darius said as he caught a glimpse of a camouflaged *Atrociraptor* approaching through the bushes.

Darius eyed the approaching *Atrociraptors* and Kenji's car. He and Kenji were close enough to the car, he thought. Maybe they could make it.

Then Darius saw the guard start to make his rounds, unaware of the danger. Darius tried to warn him, but it was too late. One *Atrociraptor* bolted for the guard and took him down. Then another sprinted right past the fallen guard, headed for Darius.

But he, Kenji, and Mr. Kon were already going for the car. While Kenji fumbled for his keys, they heard a loud click. Mr. Kon had stepped over the security perimeter, triggering his ankle monitor. All around the property, red lights were activated, and an alarm sounded!

The noise startled Kenji, who dropped his keys in the grass. As he ran back to get them, an *Atrociraptor* took notice and chased him. Kenji got the keys but found his path blocked by the ferocious dinosaur. As it reared back to attack, no one was more surprised than Kenji when Mr. Kon jumped in front of him!

There was nothing Kenji could do as the dinosaur clamped its jaws on Mr. Kon's shoulder.

"Run, Kenji!" Mr. Kon shouted. "Run, Son!"

Father and son locked eyes as time seemed to stand still.

It was only Darius's voice saying "Kenji, we gotta go!" that got Kenji moving again.

The two boys ran to the car and stopped in their tracks when they saw that all of Kenji's tires had been slashed.

Then they heard the now-all-too-familiar high-pitched whistle and saw the *Atrociraptors* look up and run toward them. This time, Darius was able to follow the noise to a nearby water delivery truck.

A thin woman with facial scars stepped out of the truck and opened a side door. Darius and Kenji watched in horror as the white *Atrociraptor* leaped out. Then the woman blew the whistle again, and all three *Atrociraptors* bore down on the boys.

The terrible tension was interrupted by the blare

of a car horn as the vehicle pulled up, placing itself in between the boys and the dinosaurs.

A door opened and a voice shouted, "Get in!"

Darius and Kenji leaped inside as the car took off in a cloud of dirt. Darius looked out the back window, determined to find out who the mysterious woman was and what she was doing there . . . no matter what it took.

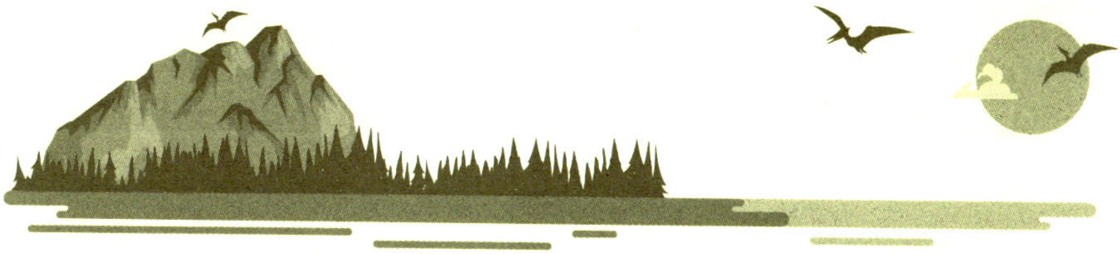

CHAPTER TEN

During practically the whole road trip with Ben, Sammy had been trying to reach Yaz on the phone. To make sure she was actually home. To make sure she was still . . . alive.

When she finally heard Yaz's voice on the other end of the phone, she nearly rolled out of the van. Yaz had actually picked up!

"Hi!! It's so good to hear your voice! It's been a while!" Sammy shouted.

Yaz said she had been busy with school, while Sammy quickly explained that she was with Ben, and they were coming to see her. In about an hour.

When Yaz asked why they were coming, Sammy didn't answer. They exchanged "I love you's" and hung up.

His eyes on the road, Ben said, "So, you didn't want to tell Yaz what's going on?"

"What do you want me to say? 'Hey, Yaz! You know all those dinosaurs you've been traumatized by? Well, guess what. Now you and all your friends are being hunted by them.'"

"Hmm . . . good point."

Looking out the window at the highway rolling by, Sammy said, "I don't know how she's going to take the news about Brooklynn being targeted. We just gotta ease into this stuff. The last thing I wanna do is bombard her with bad news. Remember how she got when the dinosaurs made it to the mainland?"

"Her PTSD is still affecting her that badly?" Ben asked, his voice full of concern.

"Well, to tell you the truth, we haven't really talked much lately," Sammy said. Yaz had been so busy, and Sammy could tell that her girlfriend was putting up a front, pretending that everything was fine. But Sammy knew better. She felt like Yaz was struggling.

An hour later, Ben's van crossed a bridge over a lake, driving up to a large metal gate. They looked at the closed gate and made note of two cameras that were blinking red.

"I knew this was a protected island, but this security seems a little over-the-top, don'tcha think?" Sammy said.

"After everything we've seen, 'over-the-top'

doesn't seem so bad."

A moment later, the cameras lights changed from red to green. With a loud CA-THUNK, the gate opened. Ben drove forward, passing a sign that said DINOSAUR-FREE ZONE.

"Here's hoping," Ben said as the gate closed behind them.

Yaz was waiting outside her apartment, nearly jumping up and down with excitement as Ben pulled up. Sammy hopped out of the van and barreled toward her.

"I've missed you so much!" Sammy said as the two kissed.

"I've missed you, too," Yaz said.

"So this place is *really* dinosaur free? Like . . . *no* dinosaurs?" Ben asked.

Yaz smiled at Ben, then looked at his van. "Judging by the look of *that* thing, I'd say we've got *one* now."

"Hey! My van isn't old, it's *classic*."

"The whole thing's being held together by duct tape," Sammy said. "It's old."

The friends laughed like they hadn't a care in the world. Yaz hugged Ben, and for a moment, everything was fine.

"Okay," Yaz said. "Who's hungry?"

"Actually, I know this doesn't make a lot of sense, but we really need to get going," Sammy said.

"Get going? But you just got here!"

"No, *all* of us. That includes you," Sammy stated.

"I can't just leave, I—" Yaz shook her head. Confused, she finally said, "Okay, Sam. What is going on?"

Like a parent talking to a child, Sammy put her hands on Yaz's shoulders, and in a calm voice, said, "Everything's gonna be okay, but . . . there are some . . . dangerous people that are looking for us. All of us. Kenji and Darius, too. We came here as soon as we could to get you."

"So . . . the Camp Fam is in danger?" Yaz said.

"Exactly!" Sammy said, relieved that Yaz understood. "Let's get going!"

Sammy started to pull Yaz toward the van, but the other girl resisted.

"Whoa! Wait, let's just think about this for a sec. If we're in danger, we shouldn't *leave.* We should *stay,*" Yaz said.

Sammy explained that they couldn't stay because they had to rendezvous with Darius and Kenji."And then what?" Yaz asked. "Look for someplace safe, right?"

Sammy shrugged.

"What could be safer than an island designed

to keep danger out? Look, I get it. I was dubious at first, too," Yaz said. "But it's real." She could tell from both Sammy's and Ben's expressions that they were unsure.

"Come on, I'll show you what I mean," Yaz said.

She led Sammy and Ben to a tree-lined park, where they walked down a path while kids played, their parents watching nearby.

"So this is like . . . a therapy island?" Ben asked.

"Kind of!" Yaz agreed. "We actually help people learn how to work through their trauma so they can reintegrate with society."

"How can you possibly *guarantee* no dinosaurs make it over here?" Ben probed.

"Ohhh ho ho, let me show you, Benny boy!" Yaz said as she pointed toward something. "Ba-boom! Cameras at all the access points. Probably saw those coming in. They've even got thermal detection to alert us if a dino gets anywhere close."

Ben stared at the cameras and gave Yaz a look that said "All right, all right, not bad . . ."

But that was just the beginning of the security features. Yaz said that the island had motion-sensor lights, high-frequency deterrents, and alarms. They even had a radar system designed to detect—and *deter*!—flying reptiles.

Ben shuddered. After his experiences, "flying reptiles" weren't his favorite.

Reaching down to the ground, Yaz touched the petals of a pretty flower. "We also use West Indian lilac. Dinosaurs get sick if they eat it, so they tend to steer clear."

"Yaz, this place . . . the real world doesn't look like this," Sammy said. "Isn't this just building a false sense of security? People need to *face* their problems, not hide from 'em."

Yaz nodded. "And we're not hiding! People are gaining tools in a safe environment so one day, they *can* face their problems. In fact, I have something to show you."

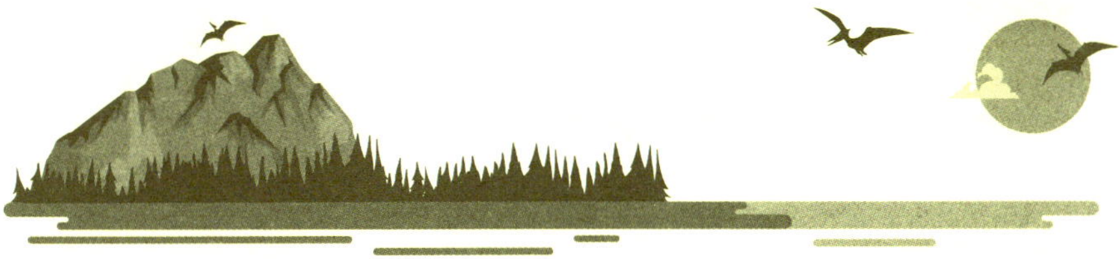

CHAPTER ELEVEN

Sammy stood on a concrete platform with Ben and Yaz, surrounded by neatly trimmed trees and bushes. Yaz ran under a pavilion, her arms outstretched, as if presenting the scene to her friends.

"The sensor's not working," Yaz said, a little frustration in her voice. "One sec."

A moment later, Ben and Sammy felt an electric jolt run up and down their spines as a *Tyrannosaurus rex* loomed over them both, its angry eyes glaring at them! They screamed as the *T. rex* roared . . .

. . . until it suddenly stopped and fizzled out of focus, only to be replaced with a *Ceratosaurus.* Then a *Brachiosaurus* . . . and a *Carnotaurus,* and a *Stegosaurus.*

It was a hologram!

"This is the project I told you about!" Yaz said. "It's a form of immersion therapy using a hologram system."

"You didn't even flinch!" Ben said, impressed.

Sammy saw that, too. Yaz wasn't nearly as fragile as Sammy had thought.

"Right?! That's kind of the whole point of this thing," Yaz continued. "It helps people get acclimated to being around dinosaurs without, you know, actually having to be around dinosaurs. Pretty cool, huh?"

Sammy reached for the realistic *Stegosaurus,* her hand passing right through it.

"Well, as impressive as this all is, we still really need to leave," she said urgently.

But Ben disagreed. He thought that this might be the right place to keep everyone safe.

"Are you kidding me?" Sammy argued. "You really think a fence and a few flowers are going to keep us safe from *this* kinda danger?"

"Okay, you two are being really cryptic," Yaz said. "What aren't you telling me?"

Sammy said they would explain once they were on the road, but Ben wasn't willing to wait.

"Someone is hunting us. And whoever it is, they're using dinosaurs to do it . . . just like they did with Brooklynn."

"Brooklynn?" Yaz said, her mind reeling.

"Ben, this is too much for her," Sammy said protectively.

"Sammy, please. I want to know everything you know."

Ben told Yaz about his theory that Brooklynn's death was no accident, that she had been targeted.

"I—I don't know what to say. This is a lot to take in. . . . Gosh, I can't believe this," Yaz said.

"I know! I know! I'm so sorry. I meant to break the news gently," Sammy said as soothingly as possible.

"No, I can't believe *you*!" Yaz fired back, surprising Sammy. "Why didn't you tell me?"

"Why? Because I am trying to protect you so you don't go falling back into the same place!"

Yaz seethed. " 'Fall back'? Sammy, look around. What more can I do to prove to you that I am not the fragile person you think I am? Why can't you see that I've *grown*?"

All of Sammy's frustration with Yaz came bubbling up, and she launched into her girlfriend. "Well, how could I? You've barely called, or texted. Left me a voicemail. Heck, even a letter in the mail would have been nice. Instead, you move away and leave me behind with hardly a word from you at all. And you sit here, and you blame me for not knowing how much you've grown? But *you* left me in the dark. *You* did that!"

"I did that because no matter what I do, you still treat me like a child instead of your girlfriend.

Maybe we should take a beat," Yaz said. "We can call Darius and Kenji, and that'll give us both some time to cool off."

Sammy stomped away from the pavilion as Yaz called after her to no avail.

A moment passed; then they heard a snarling sound.

"Are there other immersion stations on the island?" Ben said.

"Just this one," Yaz replied. "And the speakers are off."

"There," Ben said, pointing. Poking up from the tree line was a dinosaur's back sail. Then a yellowed creature with grotesque sharp teeth broke through the trees, letting out a blood-curdling roar.

It was a *Becklespinax,* a terrifying carnivore. And it looked hungry.

People in the park screamed, trying to get away from the creature. Yaz grabbed Ben's arm, dragging him across the pavilion. The *Becklespinax* followed.

Yaz paused under the pavilion and adjusted the hologram controls. The *Stegosaurus* transformed back into a *T. rex* just as the *Becklespinax* arrived! The carnivore was distracted, which bought everyone precious time to escape.

"How did that thing even get in here?" Ben asked.

Yaz had no idea, and gasped as she watched the *Becklespinax* take on the hologram. The dinosaur ran straight through the projection, and just like that, it turned its attention back to the people.

Ben and Yaz sprinted for the van and made it safely inside. Yaz called for Sammy—they had to find her and get out of there, now!

"Why does she have to make everything so difficult?!" Sammy complained, walking briskly over the bridge. "And then Ben takes *her* side! Ugh, why can't anyone ever think about what I—"

Sammy paused a moment, only to realize that somehow, she had walked all the way from the pavilion to the bridge leading to and from the island without even noticing.

Then came the siren, followed by a car horn. Sammy squinted as a vehicle approached, flashing its lights.

A red van. Ben's van!

And it was being chased by a frightening dinosaur!

"Get in!" Yaz yelled, the passenger door open.

Sammy sprinted toward the oncoming van. Just then, the *Becklespinax* smashed into the van with its snout. The dinosaur poked its head through a side window. Ben tried to steer away, but the carnivore wouldn't let go.

After another try, Ben dislodged the *Becklespinax* and stopped close to Sammy. He reached out the window, motioning for Sammy to get in, but the dinosaur chomped off the side mirror, threw it aside, and kicked the vehicle.

Yaz opened her door, slamming it into the dinosaur, knocking the creature away. That gave Sammy just enough time to climb inside the van.

Ben put the van in reverse and drove away from the dinosaur . . . backward!

Once they'd gone far enough, Ben put the van in drive and spun it around, and they moved forward down the bridge, leaving the island—and the *Becklespinax*—behind.

That was the plan, anyway. Except their path was blocked by another *Becklespinax*! Ben hit the brakes. They were now sandwiched between two dinosaurs on the bridge!

To her relief, Sammy spotted a truck heading their way. It was the DPW! An officer got out of the truck and headed toward the second *Becklespinax* with a tranq device. He fired, but the shot missed the dinosaur and nearly hit the van instead!

Then another DPW officer exited the truck and fired their tranq device . . . hitting the van's front tire, next to Ben! The tire went flat.

"Why is the DPW shooting at us?!" Yaz shouted.

The DPW officers continued to take aim at the van. They took out another tire as the first *Becklespinax* came after them again. The dinosaur smashed into the van, sending it into the guard rail. But the *Becklespinax* had too much momentum, which carried it over the side of the bridge. The dinosaur tried to use the van to regain its footing, which only caused more stress on the guard rail.

In a flash, it gave way, and both dinosaur and van plunged toward the lake below.

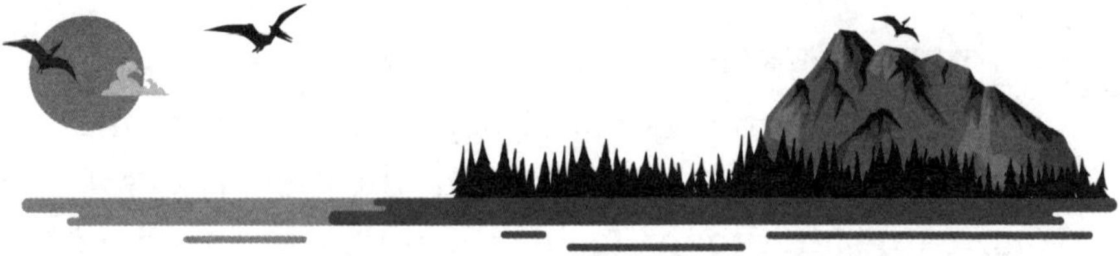

CHAPTER TWELVE

In a daze, Sammy rubbed her head as she felt water up to her ankles. Something jostled the van, and her eyes drifted toward the windshield. Immediately, two things became apparent.

First, they were underwater.

And second, so was the *Becklespinax,* whose fearsome face appeared in the windshield.

Yaz watched as the dinosaur floundered in the water. She realized that the *Becklespinax* wasn't interested in them. The animal just wanted to survive.

But before the friends could escape, the frightened dinosaur smashed the windshield with its tail. CRACK! Sammy was sure the glass would give way, and the van would flood in seconds. To her surprise, the windshield held.

Then the van rolled, sinking deeper. Sammy panicked, breathing hard as she tried in vain to unbuckle her seat belt. Yaz was there for her, though. She calmly undid Sammy's seat belt.

Gently holding Sammy's face, Yaz said, "You're okay, Sammy! We can do this, but I need you to listen to me. Okay?"

That got Sammy's attention. She took a deep breath and nodded.

The *Becklespinax* smacked into the side of the van again, its foot crashing into the windshield. The glass gave way. Water flooded through the cracks as the van sank even faster.

"Kenji? Kenji! Kenji, are you okay?"

Darius didn't know what to do. There he was, in the back of the sedan with Kenji, who seemed to be in the throes of a full-blown panic attack. He put a reassuring hand on his friend's shoulder.

Wheezing, tears streaming down his face, Kenji barely managed to say "Pull over."

Darius leaned over the seat and said to the mysterious driver, "Pull over."

"No way!" the driver said. "No way! They could be right behind us!"

"PULL. OVER!!" Darius insisted, and shot the driver a look that said "Or else."

Immediately, the sedan pulled to the side of the

deserted highway. Kenji stumbled out the door and into the night, falling to his knees.

His father . . . his father was . . . gone.

"I'm all alone," Kenji said, burying his face in Darius's shoulder.

"You're never alone," Darius said. He helped his friend back to his feet and gave him a brotherly hug. In that moment, whatever ill feeling there had been between them vanished.

"Uh . . . we really gotta get going," the driver said, interrupting. "Okay? That woman and her raptors could be on us at any second now. . . . We gotta move!"

Darius looked at the driver. He could have sworn he'd seen him before. And then it hit him.

"Whoa, whoa, wait a sec. You're from the DPW. You . . . you were there the night Brooklynn died!"

"What?" Kenji said. His anger flared, and he stormed toward the driver, slamming him against the sedan. "Are you the one doing this? First Brooklynn, then my dad?! Are we next on your list?!"

"My name is Mateo. Please don't hurt me! I swear on everything I have, I had nothing to do with your dad's death!"

"And Brooklynn?" Kenji demanded.

Holding his hands up in an "I surrender" gesture, Mateo continued. "No! I'd be dead if it wasn't for her! Please, please, just let me go. I can tell you what happened. . . ."

Kenji and Darius weren't sure whether they should believe Mateo.

"We already know what happened," Darius said. "A rogue *Allosaurus* killed her."

As Kenji slammed Mateo harder into the sedan, the driver said, "It wasn't rogue, it was there on purpose!"

"What?" Kenji said.

"Look, I'll explain everything, but we have to get back on the road before those bizarrely well-trained raptors get to us! Please!"

Considering that Mateo did save their lives, Darius and Kenji decided to take a chance. They headed back to the sedan and took off, with Mateo at the wheel.

In a desperate move to reach the surface of the lake, the *Becklespinax* kicked off against Ben's van. The move was a success, and the dinosaur sailed toward the surface.

As a result, one of the van doors popped open and the vehicle began filling with water completely! Ben, Sammy, and Yaz held their breaths before going under.

From behind the steering wheel, Mateo said, "I was a truck driver for the DPW. My job was to transport dinosaurs from point A to point B. Someone from the DPW reached out, said I could make a little overtime."

Mateo explained that he needed the money to take care of his daughter. He didn't know the name of the person he was working for—all communication was through anonymous emails and text messages. All he had to do was bring a tranquilized dinosaur somewhere and offload it to another truck. Easy money.

"I did it a few times," Mateo said. "I didn't ask, but . . . I knew all those drops couldn't exactly be legal. But at the time I thought, What's the real harm? No one's getting hurt. Until that night."

That night, Mateo said, was different. There was no other truck waiting for him. The dinosaur wasn't sedated. An *Allosaurus*. And it got loose.

Mateo hid in some bushes, petrified that the dinosaur would get him. Then he heard a woman's voice, calling out for Darius. The *Allosaurus* reacted to the sound and stomped toward the source.

Then came the scream.

He saw the woman run off, the *Allosaurus* right

behind her.

Another scream, then . . . silence.

Mateo stumbled down the road in a daze, with no idea where he was or where he was going. All he wanted to do was get away. That was when he stumbled onto the exact spot where Brooklynn must have encountered the *Allosaurus.* He saw a vibrating phone on the road. Mateo put the phone in his pocket as someone approached. He didn't know it then, but it was Darius, looking for his friend.

"I panicked when the police came," Mateo said. "They figured I was called in to *capture* the dino, and . . . I didn't correct them."

Mateo said that he remained with the DPW for a little longer, but he just couldn't keep working there. He hadn't meant for anyone to get hurt. He wanted to make things right. He'd tracked down Darius.

"I know this doesn't fix what happened, but someone should have this. Someone who cared about her," Mateo said.

He pulled Brooklynn's phone from his pocket, and Kenji took it.

"Can't get enough of that fresh air," Sammy said as the three friends collapsed on the sandy shore. She turned to look at Yaz, and they smiled at each other.

"You were great down there," Sammy said. "How'd you stay so calm?"

"I just thought, *What would Sammy do?*" Yaz said. "I guess we need *each other,* huh?"

They hugged for a moment, until they noticed Ben staring out into the lake as wet sticky notes washed ashore.

"My baby . . . ," Ben said, shaking his head sadly and thinking about his van. "Gone too soon for this world. Ciao, cara mia."

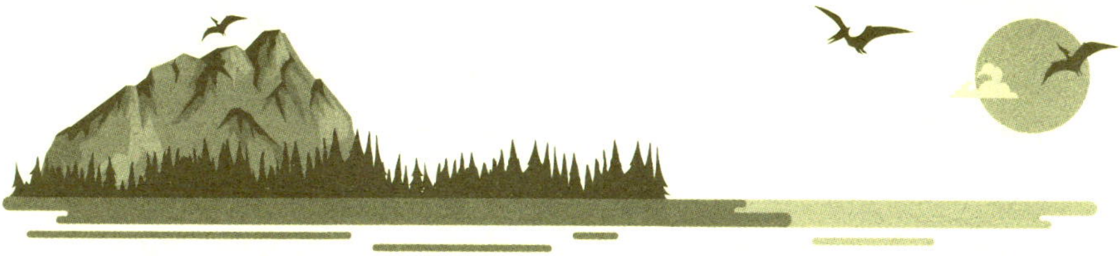

CHAPTER THIRTEEN

Kenji stared at Brooklynn's phone in the palm of his hand.

"That night . . . on the group text, Brooklynn said you two had plans. Did she tell you anything about where you were going? Or why?" Kenji asked.

Darius shook his head. "All she said was that she had something to show me."

"Any chance that phone's got a map?" Mateo interjected, startling the boys. "You know, it'd be great to find someplace safe to go. Or even know where we are."

"Yeah, let me look," Kenji said as he entered a passcode on the locked phone. "Wha . . . ?" He thought he knew Brooklynn's phone passcode, but his attempt was rejected. He tried it again. The phone buzzed. Nope.

"Let me try," Darius said. He took the phone

from Kenji, entered a passcode, and the phone unlocked. There, on the home screen, were the notifications for all of Darius's voicemail messages. As fast as he could, Darius cleared the notifications to make sure Kenji wouldn't see them. He worried how Kenji might feel if he knew that Darius had been leaving so many messages for Brooklynn.

Darius gave the phone back to Kenji, who opened a map app. They were still in Colorado. Glancing at the screen, Darius noticed a small house icon with a label that said HOME.

"'Home'?" Darius said. "Wait, Brooklynn had a place here?"

"What? No, she didn't," Kenji said. "Did she?"

According to the map, "home" was only forty minutes away.

With the van lost to the lake, and Sammy's phone—the trio's *only* phone—completely waterlogged, the friends wondered what was next.

As if in answer, there came a roar, and Yaz saw that the DPW officers were loading the two *Becklespinaxes* onto their truck.

In need of a ride and desperate to find out why the DPW had tried to drown them, Ben, Sammy, and Yaz decided to sneak aboard the DPW truck.

They overheard the officers talking about their van, and how fast it sank.

"You think those kids could have lived?" one officer said.

"Not a chance. Come on, let's get these things on the road," the other officer replied.

And just like that, the DPW rig was on the move, with three stowaways.

The sedan pulled up in front of an unassuming brick building. According to Brooklynn's map, this was the place. Darius and Kenji got out of the car as Mateo rolled down his window and said, "This is it for me, fellas."

The driver had saved their lives and gotten them this far. Besides, he had a daughter to take care of, and he couldn't very well do that if he was devoured by dinosaurs. Mateo wished them good luck and drove off.

Darius and Kenji headed inside, unlocking the front door with the code from Brooklynn's phone. It was a one-bedroom apartment with a high ceiling and a big window. Off to one side, Kenji saw a pink motorcycle helmet with flames painted on it.

As the boys looked around, Darius tried to call Sammy but got her voicemail. He left her a message warning her that something was going on with the DPW, and they might be the ones chasing the Nublar survivors.

He thought it was weird that Sammy hadn't answered her phone, but his attention was drawn to Brooklynn's desk.

"DPW press releases from Dudley Cabrera's office," Darius said, looking at a piece of paper. "He's one of the regional directors. I met him a couple of times."

He flipped through more papers and saw mentions of an escaped dinosaur . . . deceased dinosaurs . . . captured dinosaurs. He wondered what Brooklynn was doing with information like this.

Accidentally nudging the computer mouse on Brooklynn's desktop, Darius saw the screen come to life. The computer was hot to the touch. It must have been on since . . . since before Brooklynn died.

"This site is tracking the location of a bunch of DPW dinosaurs."

He took note of the website—Dark Jurassic. He clicked on the message board, and a window-popped up. A message had just come through.

" 'Asset Twelve en route to drop point, ETA midnight tonight,' " Darius read. "It's in a few hours." Scrolling down, he saw a map attached to the message, with a pin dropped at a certain location. He transferred the map to Brooklynn's phone.

While Darius searched for clues, Kenji's gaze drifted around the apartment. He seemed lost and lonely. There were no photographs of family, of friends . . . of Kenji. It was a totally sterile environment.

"It's so . . . cold in here," Kenji said.

He turned to look at Brooklynn's closet. Inside was a duffel bag.

Meanwhile, Darius continued to sift through the papers on Brooklynn's desk. He found an invoice for something called Asset 9.

"Brooklynn was asking your dad about dinosaurs showing up where they shouldn't," Darius said, trying to piece it all together. "Buying and selling . . . Mateo was doing an off-the-books transfer. Is someone *from the DPW* selling dinosaurs?"

He felt his heart race.

"It lines up! Mateo was supposedly there that night to capture the *Allosaurus,* but he was actually there to give it to someone. Probably whoever was *buying* it! I gotta tell Cabrera."

"Darius? You gotta come see this," Kenji said, interrupting.

Kneeling in front of the closet, he showed Darius the duffel bag. Inside was cash. Lots of it.

Also inside was a small piece of paper, which Kenji handed to Darius.

Here's to our new working relationship. —DK.

"DK?" Darius read. "As in *Daniel Kon*?"

Kenji confirmed that it was his dad's handwriting.

What was Brooklynn doing mixed up with Mr. Kon? How much money was in that bag? Millions?

"My dad was going on and on about me joining his legacy," Kenji said. "Maybe *this* is it, *this* was his legacy. To restart his 'empire,' my dad was buying dinosaurs. And Brooklynn . . . she was helping him do it."

Darius couldn't accept that. But the evidence seemed to suggest otherwise.

Taking the papers from Darius's hands, Kenji put them in his back pocket. Then he grabbed Brooklynn's phone off her desk.

"We should go to that drop tonight. Maybe we can find out who from the DPW is selling dinosaurs," Kenji said. "Maybe we'll find out who's been after us."

He took the motorcycle helmet and the keys with it.

Locking eyes with Darius, Kenji said, "Maybe we'll figure out what Brooklynn wanted to show you . . . or what else she was hiding from us."

Picking up another motorcycle helmet, Darius followed Kenji to the door.

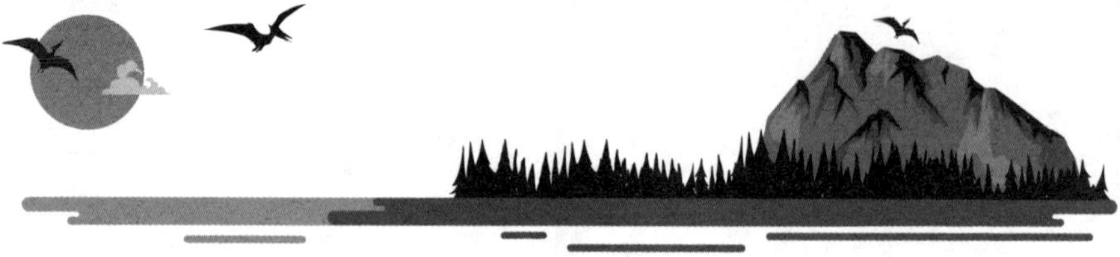

CHAPTER FOURTEEN

The problem with hitching a ride on a truck carrying two *Becklespinaxes* is that you're on a truck carrying two *Becklespinaxes.* At least the dinosaurs were sedated. But that didn't exactly reassure Ben, Sammy, and Yaz, who sat next to the creatures, practically holding their breath, afraid that the slightest movement might wake the carnivores.

Sliding past one of the snoring dinosaurs, Yaz made her way to the side of the rig. She climbed carefully on top of the *Becklespinax*'s back to get a view through the slats. But all she saw was flat land that stretched for miles. No road signs, nothing to tell her where they were going.

Disappointed, she climbed down, and rejoined the others.

Ben and Sammy were so focused on Yaz, they didn't notice that the other *Becklespinax* had woken up and was staring at them.

And then it roared.

"This definitely looks like the kind of place a shady, illegal dinosaur purchase would happen," Kenji said. Arriving at the drop site, he and Darius hopped off the motorcycles and looked around.

It was night, and they were miles away from the nearest town, in the middle of nowhere.

"The message on Brooklynn's account said the drop isn't happening until midnight," Darius said.

Kenji spotted an old shed, and the boys decided to take cover inside. It was cramped and filled with cobwebs. Rusty tools lay scattered about.

Darius looked out the small window as they waited. Trying to make conversation, he said, "Soooo . . . Brooklynn's apartment, huh?"

Kenji suddenly came to life. "A whole secret apartment! I mean, it's bananas, right?"

"*So* bananas!"

"Makes you wonder what else she was hiding from us," Kenji said, nodding at Brooklynn's phone, which Darius clutched in his hand. "Brooklynn basically lived on her phone. If anything is gonna tell us about what she was really up to, it's gonna be that thing."

Without hesitating, Darius unlocked the phone. But then he remembered the messages he had left for Brooklynn. He couldn't let Kenji see them!

"Should we really snoop on her like that?" Darius said, stalling. "I mean, it seems kinda private . . . like reading her diary."

Kenji stood, reaching for the phone. Darius managed to rise, turning away from his friend while simultaneously locking the phone again.

"Dude, we just got done rifling through her entire apartment," Kenji said. "I'd say we're a little past privacy now."

"Um . . . okay," Darius said, realizing that Kenji wasn't going to let this go. He sat back down, keeping control of the phone. "Let's see what she was up to."

The *Becklespinax* strained within the cramped confines of the rig, doing its best to devour Ben, Sammy, and Yaz.

The DPW truck unexpectedly came to a lurching halt, and the dinosaur seemed to lose interest in eating the kids. The back door unlocked and the *Becklespinax* lunged toward the opening, snapping her menacing jaws at the two DPW officers! Both evaded the creature's attack and used their stun spears to take the fight out of the dinosaur and maneuver it out of the truck.

Unbelievably, the other *Becklespinax* remained asleep. Ben, Sammy, and Yaz, obscured by the dinosaur, looked for a way out. They spotted a grate on the floor. Without waking the dinosaur or alerting the DPW officers, they slowly pried it open. Sammy went through first, followed by Yaz and then Ben.

"You seriously signed up for another of those late-night runs?" Ben heard one of the DPW officers say. "Is dealin' with these dinos even more worth the extra cash?"

"Shhhh!" the other officer said. "Maybe *don't* talk about this out in the open?"

Underneath the rig, Ben, Sammy, and Yaz heard the DPW officers wake the sleeping *Becklespinax* above. They forced the dinosaur out of the rig with their stun prods.

The trio heard a man approach, yelling at the DPW officers. "You don't need to shock her like that when she's this tranqed up. Just get her out to the field—unharmed."

Ben thought it was strange, but the man really seemed to care about the dinosaur.

"We should find a phone," Sammy whispered. "Darius and Kenji need to know we found the guys who've been huntin' us."

Swiftly and silently, Ben, Sammy, and Yaz moved

out from under the truck and headed toward the back. To one side, there was a field with a fenced-off area, and inside, dinosaurs of all shapes and sizes drinking from a lake.

"Hey!" a voice said, and the startled trio turned to find themselves face to face with the man who had told the DPW officers not to harm the dinosaurs!

Darius wasn't sure how long they'd been watching videos of Brooklynn and Kenji being cute together. It felt like days, but it had probably only been a couple of minutes.

Kenji was happy to see and hear Brooklynn again, even if it was just videos on a phone. He agreed that they could stop watching, but they hadn't checked any text messages or voicemails yet.

Hoping to dissuade Kenji from listening to them, Darius said that most of the messages were probably robocalls. When that didn't seem to do the trick, he continued, "This is crossing a line. It's too personal. It kinda feels like an invasion of her privacy?"

But he wasn't fooling Kenji. "What're you hiding?" Kenji demanded.

Darius stuttered, saying that he wasn't hiding anything, which only made it sound like he *was* hiding something.

Kenji abruptly snatched the phone and exited the shed. He was surprised when Darius grabbed his arm and said, "Kenji. Give me the phone."

Kenji refused, and the two actually wrestled each other to the ground, Kenji trying to keep his grip on Brooklynn's phone, until at last, Darius got the upper hand—and the phone. He shoved his friend to the ground.

"Darius . . . what's going on?" Kenji asked, his voice almost gentle.

Without saying a word, Darius pressed the voicemail icon on the screen and threw the phone to Kenji. Then he went inside the shed.

Puzzled, Kenji looked at the phone and pored over the voicemail messages. They were all from Darius. And all had been left after Brooklynn died.

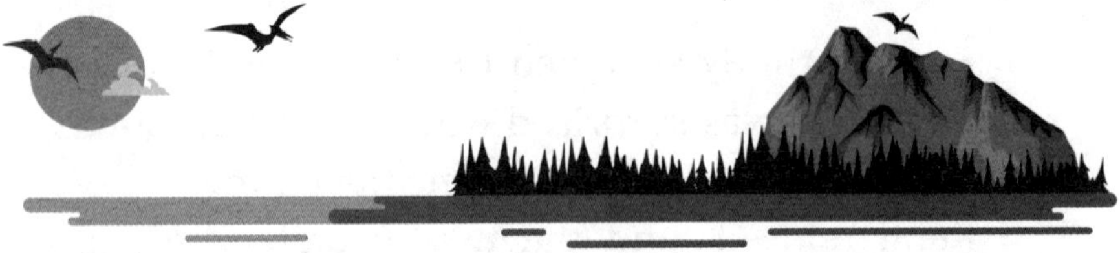

CHAPTER FIFTEEN

"Hey! Civilians aren't authorized to be here," the man said. "Hold on a sec . . . I know you. You're part of the Nublar Six. What's going on? Is Darius with you?"

"How do you know Darius?" Ben said.

"Know him? I hired him," the man replied. "I'm Dudley Cabrera."

"Aren't you, like, the DPW boss?" Ben asked.

"*A* boss," Cabrera clarified. "Regional director. This is my region."

Unsure if they could—or should—trust Cabrera, Yaz decided to go for broke. "Well, *boss,* two officers from *your region* tried to kill us."

"What are you talking about?" Cabrera said. He seemed genuinely shocked.

"Those guys who just showed up with the two dinos ran our van off a bridge," Sammy explained.

"Jared and Jensen?" Cabrera said. "Why would they want to hurt kids?"

"Adults," Ben said, folding his arms.

"You had nothing to do with it?" Sammy asked.

"No way," Cabrera answered. "Here, come with me. We can go someplace safe, figure out—"

Cabrera started to herd the trio away from the fence, when Sammy whirled around, sweeping Cabrera off his feet.

When he stood up, Ben, Sammy, and Yaz were gone.

And so were his keys.

Kenji went back inside the shed and saw Darius lying quietly in an old bathtub, just staring at the ceiling.

"Darius? These voicemails . . . all from after she died," Kenji said. "There are hundreds of them. What aren't you telling me, man?"

Darius could feel the courage ebbing and flowing within him, an ocean of emotion. At last, he said, "I was in love with Brooklynn."

"What?" Kenji said. "When did you . . . ? When she and I were . . . ?"

"No!" Darius said, sitting up quickly. "Never! I promise. I didn't even start feeling that way until after you broke up with her. I didn't even think I *could* feel that way. But when she came to stay with me, things started to change."

Kenji looked at the phone, and he handed it back to Darius.

"So my best friend fell in love . . . with my ex-girlfriend," Kenji said. "Did she love you back?"

Darius didn't answer. He just stared at the phone in his hands as his eyes went wide.

"Darius?" Kenji prodded.

"Brooklynn called me the night she died, left a couple voicemails but . . . there's an unsent message here. It's a video," Darius said.

"This way!" Ben said as the friends ran through a maze of cargo containers.

"Is that Cabrera dude in on this, or just really bad at his job?" Yaz wondered aloud.

"Either way, we shouldn't trust him," Ben said. Shaking the keys in his hand, he added, "But he did seem pretty oblivious to me. One of these should get us into an office or something. There could be info about why two random DPW officers are after us."

"Or at the very least, a phone so we can warn Darius and Kenji," Yaz said.

Nodding at one another, the trio noticed a trailer up ahead. Advancing toward it, Ben heard the familiar bellow of a dinosaur.

"Bumpy!" Ben and Sammy exclaimed. And as Yaz raced over to join them, she saw the *Ankylosaurus* inside a container.

"Don't worry," Ben said. "We're gonna get you out of here."

Bumpy bellowed again and pawed at the ground.

"She never did like bein' locked up," Sammy observed. "But this is *different.*"

Yaz glanced at a chart attached to the side of the trailer. An unsettling entry showed that Dino 7 was "deceased."

But Bumpy wasn't dead! What was going on?

"What if they did something to Bumpy?!" Ben cried.

Bumpy whacked her tail against the side of the crate as Ben searched for the key that would unlock it. The sound of footsteps caused Sammy and Yaz to look around the corner. Jared was heading their way with a tranq device!

"We got this," Yaz said to Ben. "You get Bumpy."

Sammy and Yaz waved at Jared. The pair rain away from him, and Jared gave chase. He didn't notice Ben crouching in the shadows near Bumpy's container.

"I've tried calling you, texting. I even left you voicemails. You know how much I hate leaving voicemails, so you know this is important!" Brooklynn said.

Headlights flash. A car passes by. Brooklynn hesitates. "You said you'd be here. I'm worried, Darius."

Standing up, Brooklynn walks for a moment, shouting, "Darius, where are you?!"

Suddenly, she stops. Heavy sounds. Ground rumbling. A look of fear falls on her face.

A spine-tingling roar.

The Allosaurus, *appearing behind her.*

Brooklynn, running. Stopping. Seeing something. Something even more frightening.

The sound of a whistle.

The phone falls. Brooklynn screams.

The end.

As they finished watching the video, Darius felt consumed by guilt. He wanted to tell Kenji why he hadn't been there for Brooklynn, but he just couldn't bring himself to do it.

Before Darius could say anything, lights shined their way. Both boys ducked below the window and peered outside, only to see two large rigs pull up. One had DPW markings, but the other was mysteriously blank. They could make out the silhouettes of two people—a DPW officer and someone else. The other figure handed the DPW officer what appeared to be a suitcase.

"That must be the money!" Kenji said.

The two figures then moved to the back of the DPW rig and opened the door. Inside were a sleeping *Baryonyx* and a *Stegosaurus.* The figures transferred the drowsy *Baryonyx* into the other rig, bypassing the *Stegosaurus.*

"I bet if we follow it, we'll find whoever's making the purchase," Kenji said.

Darius agreed, and watched as the two figures made their way back into their vehicles. Darius and Kenji headed back to the motorcycles. Putting on their helmets, the pair left their headlights off and followed the departing rigs down the road.

Sammy and Yaz ran through the corridors of cargo trailers, dodging tranq darts as Jared fired at them.

Up ahead, the pair saw a row of DPW SUVs. They tried door after door, but the vehicles were locked. At last, Sammy and Yaz found an open door and climbed inside. The keys were on the driver's seat. Yaz started the SUV and floored it past Jared.

"Woo! That was close!" Sammy said. In the side mirror, a pair of headlights appeared, and she saw

Jared following them in another SUV.

"Hold on!" Yaz said. She hit the gas, trying to lose Jared. But he wasn't about to just let her go, and stayed close behind, following Yaz at every turn.

Meanwhile, Ben finally managed to find the key to unlock Bumpy's container. He opened the door, but she refused to move.

"C'mon, Bumpy, we've gotta go!" he urged. He took cover as a pair of DPW officers walked toward Bumpy's crate.

Jared's SUV rear-ended their truck, so Yaz switched tactics. She steered toward the fence by the watering hole. She saw all the dinosaurs and said, "Wanna make a little chaos?"

Making a sharp right, Yaz plowed through the fence toward the watering hole, honking the horn to get the dinosaurs out of their way.

But none of the dinosaurs budged!

Unsure what she should try next, Yaz saw that Jared was still following them. "Plan B it is," she said.

Yaz floored it toward the watering hole. And just as it looked like she would sink the vehicle, she tugged hard on the wheel, avoiding the lake entirely.

Unlike Jared, whose SUV splashed into the water.

"Hang on, Ben, we're coming!" Yaz said, driving back toward the containers.

Stuck in the lake, Jared cursed his luck. He growled at a *Stegosaurus* that simply stared at him and said, "What're you looking at?!"

At that moment, he heard thundering footsteps and turned in horror only to witness the two *Becklespinaxes* approaching. In a panic, Jared fired tranq darts at the animals, but the device was empty. He tried to run, but it was too late. One of the dinosaurs lunged, and it was all over.

As they went to pick up Ben, Yaz and Sammy found that both he and Bumpy were gone from the spot where the container used to be. They spotted Ben a short distance away, sneaking up on Bumpy's container, which was now on the back of a DPW rig.

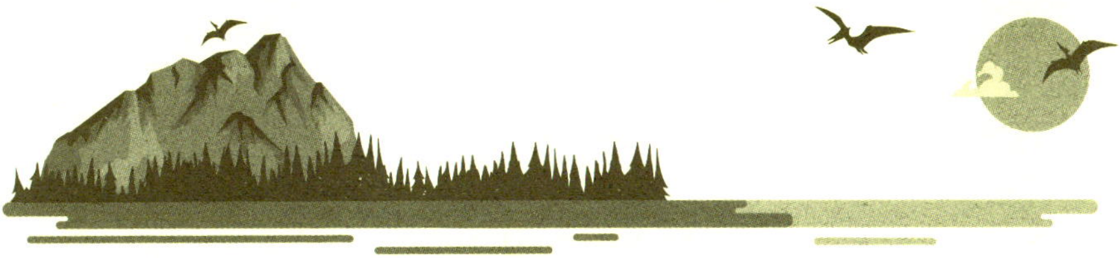

CHAPTER SIXTEEN

For a moment, Yaz wondered why her hands hurt. Then she realized just how hard she had been grasping the steering wheel of the SUV and eased her grip slightly. She was doing her best to tail the DPW rig that had taken off with Bumpy, and a stowaway Ben, when the truck drove into a thick bank of fog.

Yaz followed.

"Why'd they mark Bumpy deceased?" Sammy asked.

Yaz could feel Sammy's anxiety, and she held the steering wheel tighter again.

"What if they find Ben in there with her? Where are they even going?" Sammy said.

Doing her best to stay calm, Yaz focused on the truck up ahead. The SUV's headlights weren't much help in the fog, but then Sammy became worried that the headlights might tip off the DPW driver that they were being followed. She reached over to turn the lights off, causing Yaz to jerk the wheel. The SUV nearly went off the road!

Up ahead, the DPW had stopped. Yaz hit the brakes and switched off the headlights. Through the fog, she could make out a ROAD CLOSED sign. The DPW rig started up again and drove right past the sign like it didn't exist.

After a moment, Yaz followed.

Inside the container, Ben tried to console Bumpy. Something was bothering the *Ankylosaurus.* The dinosaur moaned and groaned.

At first, Ben thought maybe she was hungry. There was a bale of hay in the container, and Ben gave her a handful. Bumpy took a bite, then spit it out. She banged her tail against the wall and scratched at the floor. Bumpy let out a mournful sound as she whacked her tail against the wall again.

What was wrong?

Darius and Kenji emerged from underneath a parked truck as another DPW rig drove up to a security checkpoint.

"We got another one," the DPW officer said from the cab of the truck.

"All right, get goin'," the guard replied, punching in the security code that opened the gate.

Making their way through the fog, past even more DPW trucks, Darius and Kenji moved as fast as they could. On the side of one of the trucks, Darius saw a label that made his hair stand on end.

"Kenji! Look!" Darius called out.

Kenji looked over and saw the label. "'Deceased'? Why would someone sell a de—"

WHAM!

Kenji jumped back as a *T. rex* banged its head against the wall of the container. The dinosaur showed its razor-sharp teeth, breathing heavily.

"Okay, definitely not deceased," Darius said.

Kenji wondered where the dinosaur came from. There was only one way to find out, and that was to keep going. They pressed ahead, passing row after row of massive trucks with trailers. Some of them were DPW vehicles, but many others were unmarked.

Through the fog, they saw a large warehouse where workers driving forklifts were moving shipping containers. At another end was a dock—they were near water.

"There's no way this is just one person from the DPW sneaking a dinosaur out to sell," Darius said.

"And I'm guessing Brooklynn wasn't the only one buying, either," Kenji added.

"How many people are in on this?! And who's behind it?" Darius wondered aloud.

Eager to learn more, Darius and Kenji crept through the fog-enshrouded shipping yard. As they neared the warehouse, their ears were filled with the sounds of dinosaurs roaring and vehicles moving them around.

They needed to get inside unnoticed, but how? In a stroke of inspiration, Kenji suggested they try climbing onto the roof. . . .

Unknown to Darius or Kenji, Sammy and Yaz were approaching the same warehouse. As workers focused their attention on securing dinosaurs, the girls seized the opportunity to sneak inside. One of the workers accidentally dropped some tranq darts on the ground, and when they rolled near Sammy, she scooped them up.

She and Yaz snuck in through a garage door, keeping low as they forged ahead. They gasped as they entered the enormous warehouse, packed with dinosaurs of all kinds. Everything from *Sinoceratops* to *Stegosauruses, Carnotauruses* to *Ceratosauruses*—you name it, that dinosaur was here. Each was locked in its own shipping container, ready to be delivered.

On the other side of the warehouse, Sammy and Yaz noticed the rig that was hauling Bumpy and Ben backing in. Before they could head over there, they heard footsteps coming.

They ducked between two shipping containers, trying to find their way to the rig by weaving their way through the maze, but it seemed almost impossible. Every time they made a turn, they found a dead end.

At last, a familiar bellow filled their ears. Sammy knew it was Bumpy. She ran ahead, and Yaz followed.

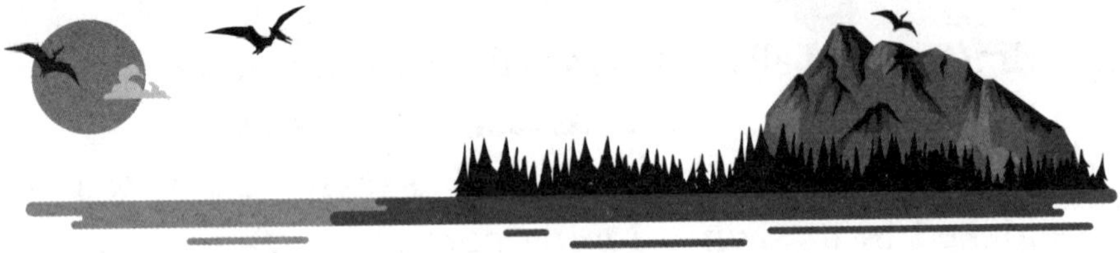

CHAPTER SEVENTEEN

In the back of the rig, Ben did his best to console Bumpy. But the *Ankylosaurus* continued to moan uneasily, almost as if she was in pain. When the truck came to a jarring halt, Ben held on to Bumpy. He could hear the DPW officer named Jensen outside.

"We gotta transfer this sick one into the shipping container quick," Jensen said. "Boss'll be mad if we lose another one. . . ."

Ben locked eyes with Bumpy, and he could see how awful his friend felt. The dinosaur fell to the floor of the container, breathing hard.

"Bumpy . . . are you . . . dying?" Ben whispered. Tears welled in his eyes as Bumpy began to cry, too.

The back door to the truck opened, and Ben knew he had to go.

"Hang in there, girl," he said as he snuck out

through the grate on the floor. Ben closed the grate behind him just as Jensen and the workers entered the trailer and prodded Bumpy away.

Above the warehouse floor, unnoticed by Ben, Kenji and Darius climbed across the catwalks in the rafters, doing their best to avoid notice. Kenji held a steel bar that he had found on the roof. Below them, they saw nothing but shipping containers and angry, unhappy dinosaurs roaring and banging against their enclosures.

"Look at this place," Darius said. "It's too big, there's too many of them. We can't take this whole operation down alone."

"Good thing we're not alone," Kenji said.

Darius had no idea what his friend meant. They were obviously alone! Then he followed Kenji's eyes and couldn't suppress the smile or laugh that came after.

"Of course they're here," Darius said.

Below them, Sammy and Yaz were making their way through the maze of shipping containers and dinosaurs!

From his vantage point, Kenji could see that Sammy and Yaz were about to run smack into a warehouse worker. Without even thinking about it, Kenji tossed the steel bar. It landed on the floor, and the worker immediately turned to see where the sound came from.

Sammy and Yaz turned that way, too.

Even Jensen seemed to wonder what the noise was.

Above him, Kenji spotted a pulley and a rope. Taking hold of the rope, he slid down to the floor. Darius grabbed the cord from another pulley and slid down after him.

A moment later, Kenji was right behind Yaz and Sammy, who had no idea who had just come up on them. Sammy whirled, delivering what would have been a devastating capoeira kick to Kenji's face if he hadn't ducked in time. He shoved Sammy and Yaz behind a shipping container to avoid detection.

"It's good to see you!" Yaz whispered.

"I missed you!" Kenji said.

Inching down the cord, Darius finally joined the others, Sammy helping him to the floor.

The four friends looked at each other, happy to be together once more.

Kenji sighed deeply, then realized—where was Ben?

Ben watched helplessly as a worker placed a high-tech lock on the new shipping container that held Bumpy. He moved away quickly, taking shelter behind a huge stack of containers to avoid being discovered.

All he could do was stare as a crane lifted Bumpy's container, preparing it for transportation.

"I'll find you, Bumper Car," Ben said. "I promise."

Darius, Kenji, Sammy, and Yaz hurried through the warehouse maze, trying to find Ben and Bumpy. Darius could feel the dinosaurs' eyes follow them.

As they moved along, Sammy and Yaz told Darius and Kenji about their experience back on the bridge, when the DPW officers shot out the tires of Ben's van, sending them into the lake.

"Selling dinosaurs and hunting us?" Kenji said. "DPW's really expanding their business model, huh?"

Kenji thought that the woman they had seen, the one with the whistle and the *Atrociraptors,* was probably a part of the scheme, too.

Sammy wondered who would want to buy so many dinosaurs.

Looking at the shipping containers, Darius saw

that each had a different label.

"I thought it was small scale at first," Darius said. "But these . . . they're going all over the world. Malaysia. The Netherlands. Saudi Arabia. Malta . . ."

The next container that Darius passed did more than catch his eye. It practically made him jump out of his skin.

Inside, he saw the milky white eye of the *Allosaurus.*

The one that had . . .

"Brooklynn might've been there that night to buy this *Allosaurus,*" Kenji said, breaking the tension.

Sammy and Yaz couldn't believe what they heard. Brooklynn would never have done that!

Kenji said, "We found an invoice and a bag full of cash at—"

"—at her *secret apartment,*" Darius interrupted.

"Apparently she was buying a dinosaur . . . from *my dad,*" Kenji continued.

"She wouldn't do something like that . . . right?" Yaz said, shocked.

"You saw your dad, then?" Sammy asked. "Is that what he said. Because he could be . . ."

At first Kenji said nothing, and Sammy noticed he had tears in his eyes. He began to stammer, trying to get the words out.

Suddenly, a figure appeared out of nowhere,

nearly running into the group.

It was Ben!

"You're okay!" Sammy said.

She tried to hug him, but Ben said, "No time! Come quick! Bumpy's dying!"

He ran off, and the others followed.

"We gotta help her!" Kenji said.

With Ben leading the way, the group reached Bumpy's shipping container. The sick *Ankylosaurus* bellowed and moaned, prompting the other dinosaurs in the immediate area to join in.

Darius and Yaz banged on more containers, causing the dinosaurs to roar even louder. Ben took advantage of all the noise to use Kenji's steel bar to attempt to pry open the lock on Bumpy's container.

But it wouldn't break.

Even with everyone joining in, the lock simply wouldn't open.

Bumpy let out a sound of pure agony, and Ben rebounded. With all the strength in his limbs, he leveraged the bar against the lock, until finally, it broke.

Ben and Sammy went inside as Bumpy collapsed, closing her eyes.

"Maybe she ate something poisonous?" Ben said.

"She could have picked up a virus!" Sammy suggested.

Then it hit them both.

"Wait . . . is she . . . ," Sammy said. "Quick, get her water! We gotta hurry!"

"Sammy, what's happening?" Yaz asked anxiously.

"Move her tail!" Ben said as Bumpy bellowed once more.

Then the dinosaur became silent.

Ben started to sob as Sammy leaned on his shoulder.

"Is . . . is she gone?" Darius said.

Still crying, Ben turned to Darius, and he was . . . smiling?

In his arms, Ben held . . . an egg.

"Looks like we've got a new Camp Fam member, y'all!" Sammy said.

Bumpy wasn't sick at all . . . she was having a baby!

Ben held the speckled egg as the friends continued to celebrate the new arrival. They didn't even the notice the shadow that fell over them. The group jumped when they heard a stun prod coming to life.

Standing in front of them was Cabrera, stun prod in hand, his formerly friendly grin now full of menace.

"Oh good, you're all here," Cabrera said.

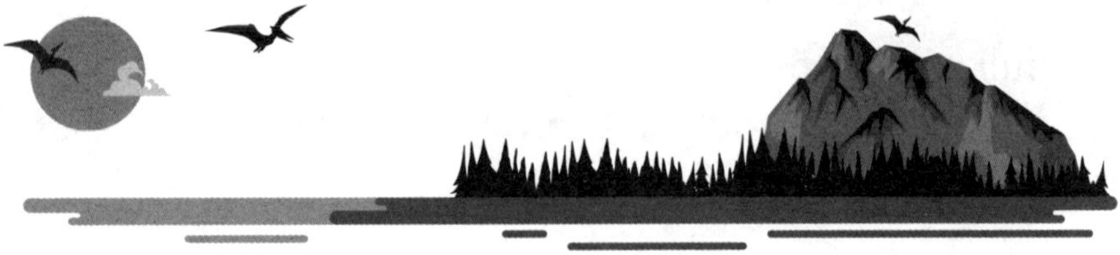

CHAPTER EIGHTEEN

"Cabrera?!" Darius exclaimed. "You're the one behind all this?! You're *selling dinosaurs*?"

Darius could scarcely contain his anger. He had trusted Cabrera. This was betrayal, pure and simple. Without regard for the stun prod in Cabrera's hand, Darius advanced on the man.

"The DPW is supposed to protect people from dinosaurs," Darius said. "But apparently everyone just needs protecting from *you*."

"Hey, I don't *want* anyone to get hurt," Cabrera said.

Eying the device in Cabrera's hand, Darius said, "That weapon says otherwise."

"Do what I say and you'll be fine," Cabrera replied. The prod didn't move.

"Is that what happened to Brooklynn?" Kenji said, standing next to Darius. "She didn't do what you said, so you killed her?"

"I didn't even know she was the one buying at first, okay?" Cabrera said. "She hid her identity. When I found out who she was, I tried to back out of the deal. Selling to an investigative journalist from the Nublar Six *and* the disgraced ex-CEO of Mantah Corp.? Yeah, no red flags there."

There was no denying it now, Darius thought. Brooklynn really had been in business with Mr. Kon.

"But she just wouldn't let it go," Cabrera continued. "The *Allosaurus* was supposed to scare her a little. Send a message. Get her to stop."

"Is that why you sent those *Atrociraptors* and their creepy . . . handler after us?" Darius demanded. "To send *us* a message?"

A look of bewilderment crossed Cabrera's face. "*Atrociraptors?* What are you talking about?"

Darius slammed his hand against the side of a shipping container in anger. "Don't lie to us!"

Cabrera moved the stun prod toward Darius. "Hey, relax. I'm the one with the stun prod here."

"You don't 'send a message' with dinosaurs unless you want someone to get hurt," Darius said.

"Well, I tried sending *actual* messages, but they didn't deter any of you," Cabrera insisted.

The color drained from Ben's face as he realized what had happened. "You're the one who sent those threats on Dark Jurassic?"

"Like I said, I don't want to have to hurt you. But if it comes down to choosing between this operation I've built or telling a story about the famed Nublar Six, so troubled, traumatized, and obsessed with dinosaurs that they broke into a secret government holding facility and tragically got eaten . . ."

As Cabrera ranted, Sammy and Ben exchanged looks. Sammy had something in mind.

". . . well, you know which one I'll pick. I've done it before, so we know it'll work," Cabrera finished.

"You say you don't want to hurt us?" Sammy said, taking the lead. "Fine. Then what *do* you want?"

"Stay out of my business," Cabrera said. "No more snooping around. You know I can find you, no matter where you are."

While Sammy kept Cabrera's eyes on her, Ben backed away toward Bumpy's container. Seeing this, Yaz moved toward Cabrera.

"We can do that," Yaz said. "I know I for one never want to be anywhere near you again."

Unnoticed by Cabrera, Ben entered the container and put the egg down next to Bumpy."Except Darius," Cabrera said. "I want him back working for the DPW. Gives us credibility. And lets me keep an eye on him. And the rest of you."

Without warning, Ben shouted, "NOW!"

Immediately, Sammy and Yaz went to the

right while Darius and Kenji ducked left. Ben leaped forward, tackling Cabrera's knees. But Cabrera wouldn't be taken down easily. Recovering fast, he caught Ben on the shoulder with the stun prod.

Ben was out of commission for the moment, so Darius and Kenji came to his aid. Sammy kicked the stun prod away from Cabrera—and then she kicked *him*! The man hit the side of a container and fell to the floor.

Moving away from Cabrera, Ben said, "We gotta get Bumpy out of here."

"And then we gotta take this whole illegal operation down," Darius said.

Ben was still recovering from the effects of the stun prod. Kenji helped his friend move through the warehouse with the group. As he did, he asked the others how they would go about stopping Cabrera.

"We go to someone higher up than Cabrera?" Darius said. "Maybe my old boss Ronnie knows who we can talk to."

"Darius, how can we be sure Ronnie's not in on it, too?" Yaz said.

Unfortunately, that was a really good point. Darius wasn't sure. But there had to be someone they could trust. He *needed* there to be someone they could trust.

Reaching an exit, Darius pulled on the door. It didn't open.

Yaz tried another exit, but that door wouldn't open, either.

Kenji approached a third exit, not noticing that the sounds of dinosaurs in the warehouse seemed to have faded. When he yanked on the door, it wouldn't budge.

"Seriously, *none* of these doors work?!" Kenji said in frustration.

"That's a heckuva coincidence," Ben mused.

"Unless it's not," Darius said.

Now there was only one door left to try—the huge garage door at the front of the warehouse. Almost as if on cue, the door opened, and the Nublar Five quickly hid. Darius, Ben, and Sammy dashed behind some crates, while Kenji and Yaz snuck into a shadowy space between two containers.

Darius could see someone step inside. It was the woman they had seen with the *Atrociraptors,* the one with the whistle.

A moment later, Cabrera stumbled into view. He seemed surprised to see the woman, and walked toward her.

"What are you doing here?" Cabrera said angrily. "I told you to stay away. I'm not cleaning up any more of your messes!"

The woman didn't say a word. She just turned her head, slowly, and stared at Cabrera.

"I-in fact, this isn't working out," Cabrera stammered. "You're fired."

Then Jensen approached, carrying a big protective case.

"Oh, Jensen," Cabrera said. "Perfect timing. Escort our friend here out."

Jensen looked at Cabrera, locking the case in his hands. Then he stood next to the woman, practically sneering at his boss.

"You really think you're the one who's been calling the shots this whole time?" Jensen said.

Darius watched as the woman put the whistle to her mouth. The sound that came out wasn't the now-familiar high-pitched frequency that drew out the *Atrociraptor.* No, this one sounded just like . . . just like the whistle he and Kenji had heard on Brooklynn's last video.

A moment later, running footsteps could be heard as the three *Atrociraptors* appeared in the warehouse. They came to a stop right next in front of the woman.

"Wh-what are those?" Cabrera said, taking a step back. "You have trained raptors?!"

"Gets the job done much better than leaving it to chance with an *Allosaurus,*" Jensen said.

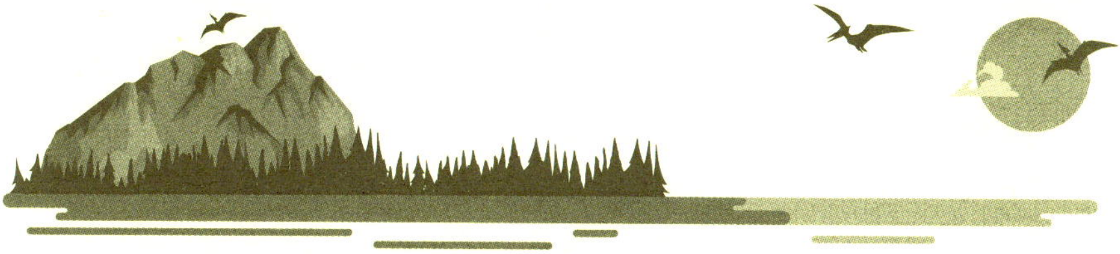

CHAPTER NINETEEN

"You killed that girl on purpose," Cabrera said as he gestured toward the *Atrociraptors.* "With those! I never would've—"

The woman glared at Cabrera as she leaned over to Jensen. She whispered something to him, and Jensen nodded.

"Got it," Jensen said as he walked away. He hit the button that controlled the door, and it slowly closed.

"Wh-what'd she say?" Cabrera shouted in fear.

Looking over his shoulder, Jensen said, "She said our boss doesn't like loose ends."

Jensen was gone, and the woman blew the whistle: a quick, short blast, followed by one longer note.

The *Atrociraptors* came to horrible life, sprinting toward Cabrera.

Cabrera ran.

Only too late did he realize that the *Atrociraptors* were herding him through the warehouse, toward the center. There, they circled around Cabrera, the Nublar Five watching in terror as the dinosaurs pounced on the man.

The woman turned toward an exit. Just as she was about to leave, she noticed that one of the *Atrociraptors* was sniffing the air around it. Like it had caught a scent. The woman stood still, taking in her surroundings.

Darius, Sammy, and Ben stayed perfectly still.

Finally, the woman gave one short and one long blast on the whistle. The *Atrociraptors* roared and started to run.

Darius knew exactly where they were headed.

"Move!" he screamed. The trio took off as one of the *Atrociraptors* jumped atop some crates to pinpoint the humans' location.

In one swift motion, Darius shoved the bottom crate. The stack toppled over, and the *Atrociraptor* went with it.

As Darius, Ben, and Sammy ran away from their attacker, Yaz and Kenji had their own *Atrociraptor* to deal with. It wedged itself between the two containers, trying to get to its prey, but got stuck as Yaz and Kenji moved backward.

With the predators temporarily preoccupied, everyone climbed a ladder to the catwalk above the warehouse and regrouped.

The woman blew into her whistle again, and this time, the white *Atrociraptor* came for the Nublar Five. The creature ran, leaping atop container after container, climbing higher and higher, until at last it reached the catwalk, blocking their path!

Down below, another *Atrociraptor* waited, showing its razor-sharp teeth.

Darius felt for the stun prod.

Sammy held one of the tranq darts she had pocketed earlier.

Darius looked down and saw the woman with the whistle watching them. She was just about to give another blast when the catwalk started to shudder.

The sound of a car horn filled Darius's ears, and he whipped his head around just as a big rig crashed right through the warehouse wall!

For a moment, everything went black. The next thing Darius knew, he was on the ground. Rather, part of the catwalk was on the ground, and him along with it!

All around Darius, containers and crates lay askew. Somehow, he got to his feet, and was relieved when he saw that his friends were all right!

As the dust settled, Ben noticed a shadowy figure holding a tranq device coming their way.

Then, a familiar voice. "Are you okay?"

It was Mateo!

"I saw those raptors coming at you through the window. Sorry, this was the best I could do on short notice," Mateo said.

"Why? Why'd you come back?" Kenji asked.

"I realized . . . I wouldn't have been able to face my daughter if I left you kids hanging like that," Mateo said. "I also *maaaay* have called the big wigs to come raid this place."

Darius couldn't believe it. He had desperately needed to trust in someone. And that someone was standing right here.

Suddenly, a dinosaur burst from all the debris. It was a *Baryonyx,* and it was not happy. It thundered toward the Nublar Five and Mateo. Everyone ran toward the rig, ducking under it to avoid the angry dinosaur.

Looking outside toward the dock, Darius could see the chaos. Workers were running for their lives as dinosaurs ran free. A *Pachyrhinosaurus* ran into one worker, sending them into the air. Other workers attempted to tranq a deadly *Carnotaurus,* with no effect.

And then Darius caught sight of the three *Atrociraptors.* They had regrouped. No doubt they would come for the Nublar Five again.

The group knew they had to keep their heads down and stay silent.

The chaos continued as the *Baryonyx* attacked the *Pachyrhinosaurus.* Then the *Carnotaurus* joined in, its reptilian sights set on the *Baryonyx.* The fearsome predator smashed the *Baryonyx* into the side of an immense shipping container. The impact jarred loose the lock, the door began to open . . .

. . . and out stepped a *T. rex.*

The dinosaur roared as it knocked over gas canisters with its massive tail.

The gas canisters exploded.

The great dinosaur stomped toward the rig as the friends and Mateo tried to run.

Only, they couldn't run. The *Atrociraptors* had found them.

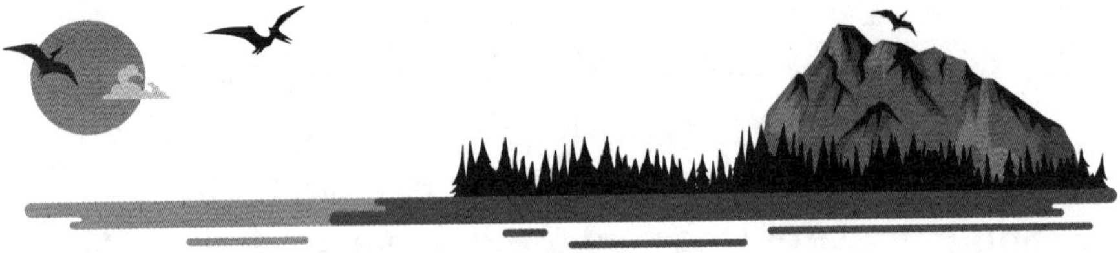

CHAPTER TWENTY

With no time to form a plan, the group split up. Kenji, Ben, and Mateo went one way, climbing atop a container, but an *Atrociraptor* followed. They didn't know whether to be relieved or terrified when the *T. rex* appeared, knocking the *Atrociraptor* aside.

Down below, Sammy was looking for Yaz as she faced off against another *Atrociraptor.* She tried to hit the dinosaur with a tranq dart but missed. Things weren't looking good.

"Hey, Stripey! Leave my girl alone!"

It was Yaz! She distracted the dinosaur as it changed direction and headed toward her.

Just as the predator leaped for Yaz, Sammy's tranq dart found its mark. The *Atrociraptor* hit the ground. The dinosaur thrashed around, twisting, turning, trying to get at Sammy. She gave it a well-timed capoeira kick to the face.

Sammy threw herself into Yaz's arms, and the couple ran.

On the dock, Darius had his own problems. The white *Atrociraptor* dogged his every move. Lucky for him, the *T. rex* stumbled his way. The dinosaur chasing Darius broke off and went after the *T. rex.* Soon, all three *Atrociraptors* were taking on the *T. rex.*

They were also blocking every escape route. Darius had to do something—but what? Looking around, he spotted a container that he recognized.

It was the container with the *Allosaurus.*

While the *T. rex* raged against the *Atrociraptors,* Ben, Kenji, and Mateo were forced to flee from their hiding spot. Sammy and Yaz retreated, an *Atrociraptor* glaring at them. Darius stared at the stun prod in his hand. He had an idea.

A moment later, Darius came charging toward the dinosaurs, the stun prod held aloft. Behind him was the *Allosaurus.* He had freed the creature from its container!

He threw the stun prod at the *T. rex* and the *Atrociraptors,* and the *Allosaurus* followed. Soon, it let out an earsplitting roar and entered the fight. The smaller predators backed off, momentarily forgetting about the *T. rex.* This would prove to be their undoing. The *T. rex* latched its jaws onto the tail of one *Atrociraptor* and flung it into a container.

The white *Atrociraptor* jumped onto the *T. rex*'s back, trying to stop it. Angered, the *T. rex* threw the *Atrociraptor* from its back and into another container. As the *Allosaurus* confronted the third and final *Atrociraptor,* the *T. rex* stalked off into the night.

At the edge of the dock, Darius regrouped with Ben, Kenji, Sammy, Yaz, and Mateo. Hiding behind a crane, they continued to watch the predators take each other down.

Darius noticed Jensen nearby, still holding the large protective case, and wondered what he was carrying.

"We don't have time to load them all, but we gotta get something to the Broker or heads will roll!" Jensen shouted.

"The Broker?" Darius said aloud. Who was the Broker?

Jensen was on his phone, trying to get ahold of someone. Darius saw the *Allosaurus,* fighting the last *Atrociraptor.*

The smaller predator had climbed atop the larger. After a brief moment, the *Allosaurus* tossed the *Atrociraptor* aside like it was nothing.Then the *Allosaurus* saw Jensen.

"No, no, no, no, no!" Jensen said as the *Allosaurus* approached. He screamed and tried to run, but for Jensen, it was all over. The *Allosaurus* saw to that.

When the giant dinosaur finally stomped off, Darius thought things might finally be going their way.

Then he heard the whistle. One quick, sharp blast, then another, longer one.

The woman with the whistle stood on the dock, the *Atrociraptors* closing in. The dinosaurs were limping, some of the fight taken out of them from their clashes with the *T. rex* and the *Allosaurus.*

The woman with the whistle seemed to notice this, too. She looked at the dinosaurs for a moment, then gave a long whistle. They dashed right past the group and went to the woman's side. Darius was surprised when the woman actually began to pet them. Then she sent the dinosaurs away and fixed her icy gaze on Darius and the group. . . .

Sirens blared, and the woman disappeared into the night.

"Well, that was . . . unnerving," Mateo said. "But hey, looks like backup arrived just in time. I'll make sure they get these dinosaurs someplace safe . . . and away from people."

Mateo shook Darius's hand and walked toward

the rapidly approaching sirens.

Behind him, at the end of the dock, Darius heard the honking of a ship's horn. He saw a cargo vessel, its engines running.

"That boat . . . I heard that officer say it's headed to the Broker."

"You think that's the boss he and that raptor lady work for?" Ben inquired.

A part of them didn't care—they just wanted this whole thing to be over. But Ben could tell by the look the woman with the whistle had given them that she wasn't the type to just let things go. She'd be back. Which meant the Nublar Five would be hunted again.

Plus, Darius pointed out, they didn't know who the Broker was or why the individual had sent the *Atrociraptors* after them.

Yaz suggested they return to her dino-free island, maybe lie low for a while. Sammy disagreed—after all, their experience had proved that the island wasn't quite as "dino-free" as they'd like it to be.

"We can't keep hiding," Darius said, staring at the ship. "That boat is headed toward the person who put a hit on us, on Brooklynn. I know Brooklynn made some questionable choices, but she did not deserve to die. I . . . I should have . . ."

Putting a hand on Darius's shoulder, Ben said, "You can't blame yourself."

"No, Ben. I'm not. I thought it was my fault for the longest time. But now I know that . . . that's not true. But I still should have been there."

Taking a deep breath, Darius confessed. "That night . . . Brooklynn and I had plans to meet up. All I wanted was to spend time with her. And that's when I realized that I was in love with her. I wasn't even gonna tell her, but she had this way of knowing exactly what you were thinking, you know?"

Staring at his feet, Darius continued. "She tried to be nice about it, but . . . it was clear she didn't feel the same."

Kenji saw the tears in Darius's eyes and put an arm around his friend.

"I . . . I couldn't face her after that," Darius said. "I was too embarrassed. And hurt. You were right, Kenji. She needed me, and I wasn't there. You needed me, and I disappeared. I tried to hide from all the pain. But I can't keep doing that."

He didn't want to be looking over his shoulder for the rest of his life, wondering if and when something bad might happen.

"We have to find out who's been hunting us, who wanted Brooklynn dead. And put a stop to it, *all* of it. This time . . . we have to try."

Darius's friends were in for whatever he had planned.

"Let's go find the Broker," Kenji said.

And with that, the Nublar Five climbed aboard the ship.

To be continued in
Jurassic World: Chaos Theory: Volume Two . . .

JURASSIC WORLD

CHAOS THEORY